WILD BILL WILLIAMS

Welshman and gambler William Williams, otherwise known as 'Wild Bill', is no stranger to trouble. It seems to follow him like a shadow. But even as a survivor of the Little Big Horn, as he claims, he has never before had to face the kind of trouble that he finds in the town of Stanton. When the bullets start to fly and the blood begins to run, Wild Bill is never far behind . . .

JACK MARTIN

WILD BILL WILLIAMS

Complete and Unabridged

LINFORD
Leicester

First published in Great Britain in 2012 by
Robert Hale Limited
London

First Linford Edition
published 2014
by arrangement with
Robert Hale Limited
London

*A catalogue record for this book is available
from the British Library.*

ISBN 978–1–4448–2069–0

*This one is for my mother —
who taught me to read
in the first place.*

Records show that between 1850 and 1920 some 80,000 Welshmen left their native lands for America. The true figure would be much higher as Welsh people were often recorded as being English, which for some reason, did not happen with the Scots and Irish. Whatever the true figure, the fact is that there were a great many Welshmen in America during the period we now think of as the Wild West. The Welsh made their own unique contribution to the mixing pot that was late nineteenth-century America.

This is the story of one of those Welshmen.

1

There was nary a frown when Wild Bill Williams was in town. He had a way about his manner that enabled most folks to forget all their troubles and become positively festive. It was said that Bill could start off a dance at a funeral and carve a grin out of the most granite of faces.

He had been born a Welshman; in a village called *Gilfach Goch*, a name that was unpronounceable to all but himself. But as a young man of fifteen summers, with no compulsion to go and work in the coalmines, those same mines that had aged his father beyond his years, he had set out in search of adventure and found himself stowed away on a ship making the Atlantic crossing to the United States. He'd landed in New York and after a few aimless years had started out West in search of the future he had in mind for himself.

'*Go West, Young Man, and Grow Up with the Country,*' the *New York Tribune* had advised in striking headlines that had filled men such as Bill Williams with optimism for a future on the rugged frontier. It had seemed Bill's destiny to follow the westward trail. What that destiny was, no one, Bill included, knew.

Indeed, if Bill had ever known what he had intended to do with his life then he'd long forgotten. And these days he just walked through life happy-go-lucky and faced whatever fate threw at him.

Fate sure did like to interfere with Wild Bill Williams.

Take today for instance; one moment Bill was enjoying a poker game after drifting into the town of Stanton, and the next he was in the jailhouse nursing a split head.

It had happened thus:

Bill, face totally expressionless, peered over his cards at the men seated around

2

the table. He was holding, 'Aces Up', a strong enough hand but he would have preferred better. There were three men, four counting himself, at the game and Bill looked at each of them in turn. Dutch Carter had a sweat on, Sam Jessup looked to be almost asleep and Cleveland Ohio, lovely name that, sat trying to suck life into a massive cigar.

'You know,' Bill said, about to make his move when the batwings suddenly swung open and a young man of maybe seventeen summers stood in the doorway, his face furious, his hands hanging, gunfighter style, at his side. Whatever Bill had intended to say then was lost, even to himself as the actions of the armed man had stolen his train of thought.

'Caleb Stanton,' the young man said. 'I've come to kill you.'

The saloon fell silent and at the far end of the counter, a big man of about thirty, Caleb Stanton, Bill guessed, stepped forward. The big man was dressed completely in black — black pants, black shirt, black boots, with a black Stetson sat upon his head. He even wore a matching gun-belt and save for the glow of the Schofield pistol, the only colour about the man was his thick red hair, which was a trait of the Stanton clan.

'Come back when you grow up,' the man spoke directly to the kid. He seemed completely at ease but Bill noticed the way the man held his body, coiled, ready to act at any moment.

'I'm plenty growed up,' the young man said and pulled a Colt. He pointed it directly at the man named Stanton. 'Make a fight then,' he prompted.

'I'm not going to draw on you,' Stanton said, calmly.

'Then I'll shoot you down like the dog you are,' the young man snarled. 'Now defend yourself.'

'In front of all these people, I don't think so,' Stanton said and Bill had to admire his coolness. 'For the last time, boy. I'm not going to fight you.'

'You've got no guts less it's for

disrespecting women?' the young man sneered.

That seemed to hit Stanton and did provoke a flash of anger in his eyes, but it was momentary, and was immediately replaced by a smile.

'Someone been telling tales?' Stanton said.

'Fight, you coward,' the young man insisted and fired his gun, sending a bullet into the floor. 'The next one gets you.'

Suddenly the kid was pushed forward as another man came through the batwings. The newcomer, a short squat man, immediately charged the young man, bringing an elbow into the small of the kid's back and sending him sprawling. The kid lost his grip on the Colt and it clattered to the floor. Stanton immediately came across and kicked the gun away from its owner.

'Get up,' Stanton said.

Winded, the kid was unable to oblige, but it was no matter because the squat newcomer lifted him to his feet and Stanton drove a punishing fist into the kid's stomach. The kid's legs buckled and if the man hadn't been supporting him he would have fallen back to the floor. Stanton immediately followed up with a left hook to the kid's face, smashing his lip and sending a spray of blood on to the saloon counter. The kid's eyes rolled back in his head as unconsciousness overtook him.

'Ain't finished with you yet,' Stanton said and slapped the kid open handed across the cheek, reviving him.

The squat man, holding the kid, laughed.

Stanton hit the kid again and again.

Bill looked around him and frowned. The saloon was filled with folk, but no one stepped forward to help the young man; they all just stood there silently watching the kid take a beating. The kid may have started the fight but this was brutal.

'You gentleman will have to excuse me,' Bill said as the man called Stanton delivered another brutal punch to the young man's face, which was beginning to resemble raw meat. The Welshman stood up and sent his chair flying backwards, whilst immediately turning on his feet and pulling his own Colt. He stood there; legs bent at the knees, hand held rock steady with the gun pointing at the man called Stanton.

'Sit down, stranger,' Stanton warned.

'I don't think I will,' Bill said. 'And if you strike that kid once more I'll bloody well shoot you.'

Everyone in the saloon seemed to take a sudden breath.

'You new in town?' Stanton asked.

'I am indeed,' Bill answered, smiling jovially. If not for the gun in his hand he could have been greeting the other man at a social function.

'That figures.'

'Meaning?'

'Meaning you don't know how much trouble you've brought on yourself.'

'That's always the way with me,' Bill said. 'My *tad* was the same and no doubt his before him, *trafferth* wherever we go. If there's one thing a Williams seems to court, *trafferth* is it.'

There were several muffled laughs around the room, not to mention the odd sigh of astonishment but Stanton stood still, regarding the Welshman in stunned silence.

'Do you want to die?' Stanton asked, presently.

'Die? Me?' For a moment Bill seemed to be considering the question but then he smiled. 'I don't think I'm quite ready to die yet. There's still so many drinks I have not drunk and pleasant thoughts I have not thunk. The world is a wondrous place, full of possibilities so no, I do not wish to die.'

'You're loco, mister,' Stanton sneered.

'That's as maybe,' Bill said and then his voice took on a harder edge. 'Now let the kid go. Lower him down gently. I'm sure you gentlemen don't want to hurt him.'

Stanton nodded to the squat man and he gently lowered the kid down to the floor.

'Good boys, you are,' Bill said. 'Now step back from him. Go on, a bit further.'

Bill moved cautiously forward putting himself between the two men and the kid.

'Now toss your guns over, very slowly,' he ordered. 'I'm likely to get jittery and blast one of you.'

'Mister, you really do not want to be doing this,' Stanton said.

'Now there you go again,' Bill said, aware of the young man holding on to one of his legs and trying to use it to pull himself to his feet. 'Guns. I shall not ask again.'

Stanton lifted his Schofield by thumb and index finger and tossed it towards Bill.

'Now you, Shorty,' Bill said and grinned at the squat man.

The squat man shrugged his shoulders. He didn't carry a gun and had never needed any weapons other than his fists. He lifted his shirt to show he was unharmed.

'You don't carry a gun?' Bill asked, knowing such a thing was a rarity this far west.

'These are the only weapons I need,' the squat man held up his hands and made two powerful looking fists.

'*Okey-dokey*,' Bill said and without taking his gun off the two men he bent and picked up Stanton's gun. He slid it into his own waistband and then helped the stunned young man to his feet.

'What's your name?' Bill asked, allowing the young man to lean against him in order to stay upright.'

'Henry,' the young man managed, speaking through blood-soaked and swollen lips. 'I'm Henry.'

'Well, Henry,' Bill said. 'Do you think you can back out of here with me?'

'It's a whole heap of trouble coming your way,' Stanton said, but the Welshman ignored him.

'Yeah,' the kid said and regarded Bill through the tiny slits in the middle of his bruised eyelids.

'Then come on, *boyo*,' Bill said and,

keeping the gun trained on both men, he backed away, moving for the batwings.

Bill would have reached them too, had fate not decreed otherwise. But at the very last moment, Sheriff Tray Clemens came through the batwings, and in one fluid and well-practiced movement, brought the hard butt of a Peacemaker down on the Welshman's skull. And for a moment, Bill Williams had been back home in Wales, sitting upon a hilltop, his beloved Blodwen within his arms, but then there was just nothingness.

2

'How old are you?' Bill asked, rubbing the goose egg on the back of his head. He had a splitting headache, and would not have been at all surprised if the blow to the head had left lasting damage.

'I'm sixteen,' Henry said, himself speaking through swollen and stinging lips.

'Sixteen,' Bill clucked his tongue against the roof of his mouth and then wished he hadn't when the sound reverberated around his skull like gunfire. 'And whatever possessed yourself this afternoon?'

The kid stared at Bill, incomprehension in his battered eyes.

'What made you do it?' Bill asked, translating to the idiot.

'I wanted to kill Caleb Stanton.'

'I gathered that much. Why, though,

is the question?'

'He disrespected my ma,' was all the kid would say on the matter.

'You two pipe down in there,' came the sheriff's harsh voice from the front of he building. The jail-house doubled up as the sheriff's office with the cells at the rear of the building and the office and living quarters out front.

'Sheriff,' Bill shouted and immediately had to grip his head against the pain the utterance caused. He made a mental note not to shout again for some considerable time.

Clumsily, his protruding gut colliding with several items of furniture, the sheriff came through from the front of the building and stood looking in through the cell doors.

'You two ain't a nice sight,' the lawman said, then spat tobacco juice on to the floor, wiped the remaining spittle from his mouth with the back of a hand and grinned.

'I'd like some coffee, please,' Bill said. 'Strong, black and a cool compress for my head. The head you so kindly bashed in.'

'Mister, you do talk gibberish,' the sheriff said. He was a big man, both in height and girth, and aged somewhere around the mid-fifties. His head was perfectly bald and his protruding ears made him look slightly ridiculous. He had small piggy brown eyes, and a bulbous nose. Beneath that nose he wore a fine looking, slate grey moustache. 'You want coffee. I'll get you coffee.'

'*Ddiolch ch*,' Bill said and closed his eyes against the glaring daylight which came through the cell windows with all the subtlety of an old maid late for church on a Sunday morning.

'I want to thank you,' Henry said.

Bill turned his head and looked at the kid, the severity of his beating shocking him all over again. His young face looked as if a mule had kicked him.

'Think nothing of it, *boyo*,' Bill said and moaned when a fresh round of pain rebounded within his head.

'Are you a gunfighter?' the kid asked, presently.

'No,' Bill groaned some more. 'I'm a gambler.'

'You handle your guns pretty good.'

'I handle my cards better,' Bill said. 'The only bullets I'm interested in is a pair of aces in the hole.'

The sheriff returned with the coffee, filled two tin mugs and slid them beneath the cell bars.

'Drink up, boys,' he said.

Bill crawled over to the coffee and drank the mug in one go. He slid the mug back under the bars for a refill, and when the sheriff obliged he sipped the second mug.

He immediately felt a little better.

'Smoke?' he asked.

The sheriff frowned and went back through to the front and then a moment later returned with the makings. He slid them under the cell doors.

'You sure are a lot of trouble,' the lawman said.

'I don't mean to be,' Bill replied and

quickly put together a quirly. He looked around for a match, saw none and then looked again at the sheriff. And once more the lawman vanished and then reappeared with a match, which he again slid beneath the cell door.

'*Ddiolch ch*,' Bill said and drew the smoke deep into his lungs. He coughed violently and then, when his head cleared, the world seemed a much more stable place. The ground had stopped spinning, in any case.

'What gibberish is that?' the sheriff asked.

'It means, obliged,' Bill said.

'Well can't you just say what you mean?'

'I thought I had.'

'Sheriff, can I have one of those?' the kid had drained his coffee and pointed to the sheriff's makings, which were on the floor by Bill's feet.

'You old enough to smoke, boy?'

'Sure am,' Henry said, indignantly.

'Then go ahead,' the sheriff said. 'If it means you two will give me some peace.'

'What happens to us now?' Bill asked.

'You stand trial,' the sheriff said.

'For what?'

The sheriff looked at the Welshman for a moment before answering. He certainly was the oddest man he had ever come across.

'Disturbing the peace,' the sheriff said. 'Threatening behaviour, attempted murder.'

'Attempted murder?' Bill coughed and it hurt to do so. 'I didn't attempt to murder anyone.'

'Not you, him,' the sheriff pointed to the kid. 'Over a dozen people heard him say he was going to kill Mr Stanton.'

'And I'd still kill him given the chance,' the kid said, which, on reflection, may not have been the wisest thing to say.

'I'll make a note of that,' the sheriff said. 'Keep it for the trial.'

'Don't matter, no how,' the kid spat. 'We'd never get a fair trial in Stanton.'

'Would we not?' Bill asked and surreptitiously slid the sheriff's makings under his leg.

'We went up against the Stantons,' the kid said, 'in a town named Stanton, what do you think?'

Until now, Bill hadn't considered that. He'd barely taken notice of the town's name as he'd ridden past the town marker. And back in the saloon, when the kid had challenged that man, calling him Stanton, the Welshman had made no connection. His chief concern had been that his poker game had been interrupted.

'*Duw, duw,*' he said and the kid had a pretty good idea what he meant by it.

'It was Stantons who built this town,' Henry said. 'And Stantons who still run it. See the sheriff there? One of them Stantons calls and he comes running. The whole town's in fear of the Stantons.'

'Shut your mouth, kid,' the sheriff warned.

Henry ignored the sheriff. 'Everyone's afraid to go against the Stantons. They own most of the land around here and that which they do not own they

18

simply take when they get the fancy. They extort money from everyone around here. Insurance, they call it. Those that stand against them usually end up dead or vanished.'

'I won't tell you again,' the sheriff said.

The kid, though, was headstrong and ignored the lawman. 'A few people have stood up to the Stantons, but they've either suffered some kind of accident or disappeared. The Stantons pretty much do what they want in this town.'

'Oh well that's just bloody marvellous,' Bill grumbled and spirited the sheriff's makings into his own pocket.

3

'What are you taking us in here for?' Bill protested, straining against the two deputies who manhandled him towards the saloon. The Welshman's feet were shackled; the chain between the shackles was less than a foot in length, and Bill found it difficult to walk without falling flat on his face.

The sheriff, who himself supported a shackled Henry, nodded his head to a half-built structure across the town square. 'That there will be the new courthouse,' he said. 'Until it's finished we use the saloon.'

'New courthouse,' Bill said. 'Town's surely on the up.'

'Mr Stanton's paying for it to be built,' the sheriff said with a smile. 'Now come on, let's move.'

'Bloody marvellous,' Bill said as he was propelled forward and through the batwings.

Once inside Bill found himself marched across the room and made to stand in front of the counter, Henry beside him. Most of the tables and stools had been stacked in the four corners of the room, while a large oak table had been placed dead centre. A distinguished looking man with thinning red hair and wearing bifocals sat behind it. There were several chairs placed to the left of the table and all but one were occupied.

'That's the judge,' Henry whispered nodding his head towards the man seated at the table.

'That much I figured,' Bill replied. He noticed that Caleb Stanton had a smirk spread across his face.

'He's Mr Stanton the senior,' the kid said. 'His name's Abaddon Stanton, but ain't no one in town would address him by the familiar.'

'Stanton as in Stanton?'

'The same. It was he who built this town and it was his grandson I came to kill.'

'I can see we're going to get a fair trial,' Bill moaned.

'The others, that's the jury. Two of them are Stantons too.'

'Well, that's just bloody marvellous.' How many of these Stantons were there?

'Silence in the court,' the sheriff said and went and sat in the one vacant chair. His deputies went and stood each side of the two accused men. Bill noticed that their guns were worn butts facing outwards: these men were gunslingers.

The judge looked down his nose at Bill and Henry and for several moments, during which time the saloon fell deathly silent, he didn't say a word. He simply sat there regarding the two men that had been brought before him with some distaste. Finally, he steepled his fingers to his lips and closed his eyes for a moment.

'The court is now in session,' he said and then brought the gavel down on the desk with a loud bang.

The sheriff stood and nodded to the judge before clearing his throat and speaking.

'These men are here on separate charges,' he said.

'The younger man, one Henry Carthy faces charges of threatening behaviour and attempted murder.'

The judge nodded and gave Henry a stern look.

'The older man,' the sheriff continued, 'one William Williams, a Welshman, is also charged with threatening behaviour and of being a transient, which contravenes the town vagrancy laws.'

The judge looked at Bill, running his eyes from head to toe and it was plain he didn't like what he saw.

'We'll start with the lesser charges,' he said. 'William Williams, take one step forward.'

Bill looked at Henry and then did so, or at least, he shuffled forward.

'You are William Williams?' the judge asked.

'Aye,'

'You say you are a Welshman.'

'I am, indeed. And proud to be so.'

'How do you plead?' the judge asked.

Bill gave the judge a curious look. 'On which charge?' he asked.

'Threatening behaviour will do for a start.'

'Oh that,' Bill smiled. 'Not guilty and while we're at it I'm not guilty of the other, either.'

The judge frowned and regarded the papers on the desk. 'We have sworn witness statements that you pulled your gun and threatened one Caleb Stanton.'

'I only stepped in to stop this kid being beaten to death by Stanton and that ape,' Bill pointed to Caleb Stanton and his companion. 'And I didn't exactly threaten him, more prevented him from killing the kid with his bare hands. You could say, in fact, that I saved him from himself.'

Again the judge regarded his papers.

'This man,' he looked at Henry and the dislike in his eyes was replaced by hatred. 'This man attempted to kill Caleb Stanton and you defended him. Now do you make it an habit of defending killers?'

'He didn't kill no one,' Bill said.

'Only threatened to.'

'He did more than threaten,' the sheriff put in. 'Shots were fired.'

'Ah,' Bill said. 'But he didn't hit anyone.'

'Only because someone nudged his gun arm,' the sheriff again injected.

'You big *gellwydog*,' Bill said. 'He shot the floor. It was more a warning than anything else.'

The sheriff looked startled. For one thing he didn't know what the hell a *gellwydog* was and for another he didn't like the way the accused man was standing up to him. The strange Welshman knew that the judge was a Stanton and that two of his kinfolk were among the jury, and yet he was still determined to make a fight of it.

'Silence,' the judge snapped and when he next spoke it was directly to Bill. 'If his hand wasn't nudged then why did he shoot the floor?'

'As a warning I expect.'

'A warning for whom? A warning of what?'

Bill was about to answer but he

thought better of it and so he remained silent. He couldn't think of anything to say that wouldn't incriminate the kid. He couldn't very well tell the judge that Henry had been trying to provoke his grandson into a fight.

'And did you then pull your gun, Mr Williams?' the judge, realizing he had the upper hand, asked.

'I did,' Bill answered glumly and then added: 'But I didn't shoot it, mind.'

'Why did you draw if not to shoot?'

'I told you, to stop these two men, one of which seems to be your grandson, from beating the younger and much smaller man to a pulp. Didn't matter what the kid had done. He should have been taken to the jail to cool off and not beaten like a dog.'

'You intended to shoot,' the judge insisted.

'I intended no such thing.'

'Do you often pull your gun without the intention of shooting?'

'Sometimes,' Bill said and then tried to think of such an instance. 'When I'm cleaning it, maybe.'

'Do you make a habit of cleaning your guns in a public saloon?'

Bill frowned, thinking of an answer to that. 'Well,' he said, finally. 'Strong spirits are good for polishing the barrel.'

'Tell me, Mr Williams,' the judge said, changing tack. 'Where do you live?'

'In the town hotel,' Bill said. 'I'm a working gambler. I travel about a lot but I'm not a vagrant. I have more than enough money to support myself, I pay my bills wherever I go.'

'A gambler,' the judge seemed to spit the word out as if it left a foul taste. 'Well I'd say you played a bad hand coming to this town.'

'Only because the cards were stacked,' Bill said, rather enjoying the analogy.

'Guilty,' the judge said, his tone furious.

'What?' Bill asked. 'Isn't that for the jury to decide?'

'Guilty,' the judge repeated. 'You will be sentenced later. The other one, step forward.'

'Guilty of what?' Bill asked and one of the deputies slapped him across the back of the head.

'The other man, step forward,' the judge boomed.

Henry ignored the judge and the sheriff had to go and nudge him forward at gunpoint. Henry almost tripped over his shackles but the deputies kept him upright.

'And how do you plead?' the judge asked.

Henry looked across at Caleb Stanton and sneered. 'Guilty,' he said. 'And what's more I'll kill that son-of-a-bitch the first chance I get. I'm gonna send your grandson to Hell and there ain't a thing you can do about it.'

Bill shook his head. This may have been a kangaroo court but the kid could have at least made a play of explaining himself. Being headstrong and young seemed to go together.

'Very well,' the judge said, calmly. He regarded Henry with sheer undisguised hatred. 'I will retire for a moment to consider and then I shall return and pass sentence.' He stood and crossed the room towards the rear of the saloon.

'Don't rush on our account,' Bill said which earned him yet another clip across the back of the skull from one of the deputies. He also received a threatening look from the judge before the old man disappeared through a door into another room.

'Guess our goose is cooked,' Henry said.

'I thought it went rather well,' Bill said and then added: 'all Stantons considered.'

4

Abaddon Stanton was furious with his grandson. The old man paced the room, puffing the large cigar as he went, sending a trail of smoke into the air.

'How many times have I told you to keep things calm?' the old man asked, knowing the answer himself and not really expecting one from his grandson. 'I tell you, over and over and yet you still mess with one of their women.'

'I never touched no woman,' Caleb protested.

'Then why did the kid say you disrespected his mother?'

'Beats me,' Calab said and meant it. He had no idea what the kid had been talking about. 'The kid's loco.'

'Loco,' the old man looked at his grandson. 'Sometimes I think it's you that's loco. We've got to keep a quiet town. What happens if one of the townsfolk gets up the courage to call in outside law?'

'They won't,' Caleb said. 'Not if they know what's good for them. And besides we can handle any Johnny-Law that tries to interfere with our town.'

'You've had it too easy,' the old man said and sat himself down in the firm-backed chair besides the large fireplace. 'You've been brought up in Stanton and had things your way for too long. But things are about to change and when the railroad comes through here this land is going to be worth a fortune.'

'We own the deeds to most of the land,' Caleb pointed out, still unable to see what the problem was.

'We do,' the old man said. 'But until we've sold all that land, I'd rather not have a US marshall looking into those deeds.'

'We could handle any law,' Caleb insisted.

'Could we?' the old man smiled

wisely. 'Times have changed. The frontier is shrinking by the hour and our kind of law is at odds with the law of the land.'

The door opened and two more members of the Stanton clan entered. They were Dismas and Eder Stanton, and they both had a shock of red hair that was receding. They were in fact brothers, twins, and the old man lecturing Caleb was their father.

The old man ignored them and leaned forward, looking directly into his grandson's eyes. 'A quiet town,' he said. 'Do you understand me?'

Caleb nodded and stood, eager to be out of the room and away from his grandfather. He hoped that the entry of his two uncles meant that he would now be dismissed.

It did.

'Go,' the old man said. 'And try to stay away from trouble.'

5

'A travesty is what it is,' Bill complained, knowing that his words were falling on deaf ears but complaining anyway. 'Call that a fair trial? A shameful show is what it was.'

'You got off lightly,' the sheriff said and continued to buckle his gun-belt. 'Just think yourself fortunate.'

'Fortunate,' Bill spat the word out. 'Oh aye, it is fortunate I am.'

So fortunate, in fact that the sentence had gone thus: first the judge had asked as to the extent of the monies owned by the gambler; the sheriff had then informed the court that the Welshman had been carrying two hundred dollars on his person and a further thousand in his carpetbag, and so the fine had been set at, 'all that'. Added to the monetary forfeit, Bill was ordered out of town and told to stay out. If he ever returned to

Stanton, the judge had warned, he would be facing a stiff prison term. Hard labour.

Some fortune, thought Bill. Only yesterday morning he had been looking forward to a few days' gambling, and had a large stake to play with. And now not only had he been branded a vagrant, but he was once again without substance, on the hoof so to speak. Still, it was relative, Bill supposed. He was, after all, fortunate in comparison to the kid, who was to be hung this coming Sunday. That Bill intended to notify the US marshall at the earliest opportunity and stop the hanging was neither here nor there, for at the moment the kid was languishing in the jail-house with only a rope and a short drop to look forward to.

They couldn't get away with this. The trial hadn't even been legal. For one thing the judge should not have presided over the trial of a man charged with attempted murder of one of his own kin, and the jury had been there for mere dressing and were not considered at all as to a verdict. In fact there hadn't even been twelve jurors and although Bill only had a passing knowledge of the law, he did know that there should have been a dozen men both good and true. The silent jury at the trial had been made up of Stantons and several terrified townspeople.

'What about my guns?' Bill asked.

'Deputies will hand them over at the town border,' the sheriff said and handed Bill's rig to one of the deputies.

Bill looked at the two deputies, the same two who had guarded him during that farce of a trial. Neither of them seemed very talkative and Bill did so like to talk. Always had in fact. A bell in every tooth, his mum used to say, and would tell Bill that he had inherited the gift of the gab from his Uncle Morgan, whom it was best not to talk about.

Ahh well, Bill realized that he wasn't going to learn anything about the Stantons, and their hold on the town from the two lawmen. Indeed, it would not have come as a surprise to the Welshman if one or both of the deputies turned out to be Stantons themselves. There seemed to be a lot of Stantons in Stanton.

'Well then,' Bill, smiled at the sheriff. 'Then I think I'm ready to go.'

'You horse is outside, already saddled,' the sheriff said and then went to his desk, opened a drawer and returned with Bill's now almost empty saddle-bags. Before handing the bags over, the sheriff removed their only contents, a ball of wool and two lethal looking needles. 'What's this?' he asked.

'It's my knitting,' Bill said and snatched it and the bags from the sheriff. He placed the wool and knitting needles back into the bag and slung it over his shoulder. 'Shame I wasn't staying around, longer,' he said. 'I could have made you a nice horse blanket. I make rather nice horse blankets.'

'Get rid of him,' the sheriff said to his deputies and went and sat behind his desk.

Once Bill had been all but dragged from the jail-house, the sheriff placed his feet up on the desk, feeling the beginnings of a headache. He didn't like this at all, wasn't comfortable with what he was getting involved in. Old Man Stanton was starting to punch above his weight and the sheriff was concerned that if the old man went down he would end up being dragged along with him. It was one thing delivering the odd beating to a home-steader, getting him to sign the deeds over to Stanton and then running him off the land, but already they had resorted to murder. And now they were going to murder the kid and use the law, or rather what they called the law, to justify the hanging. The sheriff could clearly see things getting out of hand.

He could understand them wanting the kid hung; he'd gone up against the Stantons' authority and he had to be made an example of. There was far too much at stake to give folk the notion that the Stantons had gone soft. The

37

last thing they wanted was for other aggrieved town members to start challenging their rule, refusing to pay their insurances. He could understand that. Didn't much like it but it made some kind of sense. Why the Welshman had to be killed, though, was beyond him. He wouldn't be coming back to Stanton so there seemed no point to the killing. Though killed he would be — Abaddon Stanton had ordered it.

Abaddon Stanton's orders were usually obeyed.

6

'That's far enough.'

Bill pulled his horse to a stop and turned in his saddle to look at the two lawmen who rode close behind him. For the entire journey neither of the men had said a word, other than telling him to shut up, which they did several times.

'Is this it?' he asked.

'Dismount,' the taller of the two deputies said and reached around behind him and slid a spade out from his saddle. He tossed it to the ground.

Bill looked at the spade and then at each of the deputies in turn. This was pretty much what he had been expecting. 'You want me to dig my own grave, is that it?'

'Dismount,' the deputy repeated and lifted his rifle, levelling it on Bill.

Bill dismounted and patted his horse

on the side of the head. 'I won't be too long,' he said and went and picked up the spade. He looked at his surroundings for several moments, but made no effort to start on the digging.

'What are you doing?' the deputy asked. 'Dig.'

'Well,' Bill said with a smile. 'If I'm to dig my own grave, which I must say is an opportunity that not many men get, then I think it's important to choose wisely. After all, I'll be there for all eternity and I don't quite like it in this particular spot. It's almost a valley and seems rather cold — in winter the wind will come rushing through here. Now up there,' he pointed to a tree-topped hill which the dying sun was currently illuminating, 'now that would seem much better.'

The rifle sounded, dirt spluttered up at Bill's feet.

'Dig,' the deputy insisted. The other one, his partner, said nothing and might as well have been mute.

'Very well,' Bill said, resigned. 'But I

tell you if I don't rest easy then it'll be on your conscience.'

The two deputies looked at each other, said nothing and then turned their attention back to the Welshman.

'Dig,' they said as one.

The ground was starting to break up nicely beneath the spade and Bill knew that if he was going to make his move, then it would have to be soon. As a gambler he knew the odds of it working were against him, but there were times when a man had to run with chance, especially if it was his only chance.

He paused for a moment, feigning wiping sweat from his brow and used the opportunity to check the two men's positions. He figured the one closest to him, the one holding the rifle, would be the one to challenge. If it worked, and he was able to get to the man's guns, then he'd have a fighting chance. Both men had remained mounted, which was a mistake as far as the Welshman was concerned. Horses were easily spooked and even the best marksman in the world would find it difficult to hit a target from the back of a startled horse.

'Get back to work,' the deputy holding the rifle barked.

Bill bent, worked the spade into the ground and then suddenly hurled it backwards, over his shoulders, sending dirt into the air. He hit the ground, immediately rolling towards the two horsemen, startling the horses and starting them off in a frenzied dance as they tried to avoid the man rolling towards their legs. Before either of the men could react, Bill had jumped up and dragged one of the deputies from his saddle. The other fired, missed, but Bill kept hold of his man and brought a fist down on to his nose, smashing it. The man screamed and his struggles ceased as his hands went to his injured nose. Bill snatched one of the man's Colts from his holster and dived to the left, rolling away from the man, just as the other deputy fired again.

Bill felt the slug pass him by, perilously close, and he fired back at the still mounted deputy. His aim was true and the deputy's head was flung back with a spray of blood. Panicked, the horse bolted with the dead man still in the saddle.

The other deputy had recovered enough to reach for his remaining gun but Bill spotted him and levelled the Colt.

'Don't draw,' Bill warned. 'That nose'll heal but dead men don't get better.'

The deputy ignored Bill, drawing his weapon.

Bill fired and the deputy's nose was further obliterated as hot lead tore his face apart.

'I bloody well told you,' Bill said and shook his head. That was the trouble with fellas like these, they were always too eager to resort to gunplay. They seemed to think themselves unbeatable, that they would be quicker than the other man. Well there were two more men who had just discovered the hard way that they were anything but unbeatable.

Bill found his own rig in the saddle-bags of the deputy's horse and put it on, instantly feeling more comfortable with his own gun-belt around his waist. He mounted his own horse and had to ride maybe half a mile to recover the horse that had bolted. When he did find the beast, the dead man was still in the saddle, though slumped forward at an odd angle. Bill led both horse and corpse back to the other dead man.

He dismounted, picked up the spade and started digging.

'I told you this would be a cold place to spend eternity,' he said while he sweated on. 'But if you think I'm lugging you two up the hill, you can think again. You're lucky enough that I'm bothering to bury you at all. Ought to leave you to the critters.'

Bill continued to dig, chatting away to the two dead men as he toiled. Eventually he had dug a hole, which he decided was just deep enough to accommodate the two men. He wiped his hands on his pants and climbed from the hole.

'I usually charge for my labours,' Bill said and went and searched each of the men in turn. The grand total between both men was seventeen dollars, which didn't fill Bill's saddle-bags in the same way the twelve hundred had. '*Duw, duw*,' he said. 'It's a pauper's grave for you two.'

He dragged the men one after the other and threw them into the hole. Then he picked up the spade and covered them over. He muttered a few words he remembered from Sunday school and then, task finished, stood back and admired his handiwork.

It would do.

He would have to go back to Stanton, but he knew to do so before nightfall was too much of a chance, a bet no gambler would take. He had already played a wild card and he knew it didn't do to tempt fate too many times. The sun was sinking in the sky and in an hour or two it would be dark. After dark, Bill felt he'd be able to slip into town undetected. He could of course not bother and instead ride on to the next town and notify the US marshall there but he wasn't sure how far that was. And the kid was due to be hung on Sunday. Today was Friday and Bill wouldn't be at all surprised if the kid didn't reach the rope at all, but was rather shot down trying to escape. No, he had to bust the kid free, not that he was obliged in any way to the kid but Bill knew a great injustice had been served, and he couldn't turn his back on the situation, knowing the kid would be dead within days. There was also the little matter of the twelve hundred bucks.

He'd quite like to retrieve that.

The town of Stanton it was, then.

He had no other option.

Bill sighed and went to his saddle-bags, removed his knitting and sat himself on a rock. He expertly moved the needles, thinking that he could complete another square for the blanket before moving off.

7

Bill gave a slight tug of the reins and the horse stopped immediately. He shifted in the saddle, worked a cramp out of his legs and stared down at the town sign.

WELCOME TO STANTON.

Some welcome, the Welshman thought. He would have certainly given the town a wide berth had he known previously what he knew now.

'Hindsight,' he mumbled, 'is indeed a wonderful thing.'

He gently moved the horse forward, his own eyes alert for any movement as he neared the main section of the town. He saw the main street in front of him; it looked deserted. The only signs of life were the flickering lights from the saloon and the sounds of drunken merriment that drifted out of the batwings.

He dismounted and took the Indian pouch from beneath his saddle. The pouch, which was worn slung over the back and held in place by a strap that ran over the shoulders and around the chest, had been gifted him by a brave named Walk Tall on Steady Feet. It had originally been constructed to carry a bunch of arrows but with the deft use of a knife and thread Bill had turned it into a snug home for his Winchester rifle. He tightened the strap so that the pouch wouldn't sag with the weight of the rifle and then took the rifle from its boot and slid it into the pouch. He filled his saddle-bags with extra ammunition, for both the rifle and his six-shooters, and slung them over his other shoulder.

He was hoping to avoid any gunplay but sometimes, the Welshman knew, that was not possible.

He led his horse to the rear of a large barn and ground tied it. He patted it gently on the muzzle, whispered a few words in his native Welsh, and then proceeded to walk into town. As he walked down Main Street he kept his head bowed, not wanting to be recognized should anyone spot him. And armed as he was, the butt of the rifle sticking out above his shoulders, he hardly looked inconspicuous. Thankfully the street was empty and Bill reached the town newspaper and telegraph office without incident.

The building was in darkness but as Bill peered into the window he saw the flicker of a pale light coming from the back of the building. The owner obviously lived on the premises. Bill pulled one of his Colts, went and tapped the front door and stood aside, his back against the wall, his eyes scanning the still deserted street. When there was no answer, he used the butt of his gun and rapped harder on the door. Almost immediately the Welshman heard movement inside.

'Hello,' a timid voice sounded from behind the door. 'Who is it? We're closed.'

Bill said nothing, tapped the door again.

'Who is it?'

Bill cleared his throat and then muttered, 'Sheriff,' he kept his voice low. This was a small town and the Welshman wouldn't have been at all surprised if the man behind the door knew the sheriff's voice intimately. 'Open up,' he commanded and once more rapped the door.

The door opened slowly and Bill immediately pushed it, sending the man behind sprawling. The Welshman went through the door and quickly closed it behind him. He stood looking down at the small man who cowered on the floor, spectacles askew, and a thin trickle of blood at one corner of his mouth.

'Stand up slowly,' Bill said, keeping his Colt on the man.

The man did so, first getting to his knees and then groaning as he got back to his feet.

'What do you want?' he asked.

Bill regarded the man for a moment before speaking, wondering how threatening he needed to be in order for the man to do his bidding. 'What I want you to do,' he said, 'is work that contraption of yours. I want to send a telegram.'

The small man frowned; he obviously hadn't been expecting that and it was clear that being held at gunpoint and then ordered to send a telegram was a novel experience for him.

'I usually stick to opening hours,' the man said.

'Where is it?' Bill asked.

'Where's what?'

'Your contraption?'

'It's in the office, out back.'

'Lead the way,' Bill prodded the small man in the ribs with the Colt, which provoked a high-pitched squeal.

'Now what I want you to do,' Bill said, 'is to send a message to the commander over at Fort Hood. He's a personal friend of mine.'

'Really?'

'Aye,' Bill prodded the man in the back again. 'I served with him when he was merely a sergeant. Name's Nathan

Brittles and he's a bloody good man to have on your side during a fight.'

The man looked at Bill with a vacant expression. Rather than being impressed by the name of the commander he simply looked bemused.

'You want me to send him a telegram?' the man looked at Bill incredulously.

'Aye,' Bill said. 'I thought I'd made that clear enough.' He gestured once more with the Colt.

'What do you want to say?' the small man now looked more mystified than ever.

'I want,' Bill said, trying to think of the wording, 'I want you to tell him that Stanton is a rotten town and that a young man is due to be hung in what is quite clearly a travesty of justice. A murder carried out under the colours of the law. I want you to request he send some men over immediately and then notify the US marshall's office. Address it as from me, William Williams, formerly of the seventh and he'll understand.'

'All that?' the man stammered.

'All that,' Bill nodded. 'And also inform him that tonight I will bust the kid out of the jail, take control of the town and hold it until the real law arrives.'

'You intend to take over the town?'

'I do,' Bill nodded. 'And I will.'

For several moments the man regarded Bill thoughtfully. No longer did he feel afraid and now it was confusion that shone in his eyes.

'Well get that contraption working,' Bill said and holstered his Colt. There no longer seemed any need for the weapon. 'I shall not tell you again.'

'You can't put all that in a telegram,' the man said. 'And besides, at this hour there would be no one on the other end to receive the message. There's also the fact that my contraption, as you call it, is broken down. We are waiting for a part which won't arrive for at least another week.'

Bill frowned.

'Wait,' the man said, reading the look in Bill's eyes as one of danger. 'You could send a letter. A good rider on a fast horse would reach the fort by the day after tomorrow.'

'Aye,' Bill said. 'I could do that. But who would I send?'

The man smiled then, and now seemed to be regarding Bill with a look of admiration.

'Do you really think you could take control of the town?' the man asked, countering Bill's question with one of his own.

'I can,'

'But Stanton's a powerful man. He has many guns in his employ.'

'Doesn't matter,' Bill said and there was something in his voice that gave the words credence.

'You mean it?'

'I do,' Bill said.

The man held out his hand and Bill took it. They shook and then the small man smiled, 'Dave Thomson,' he said. 'Editor of the *Stanton Chronicle*, telegraph operator and general town's dogsbody.'

'William Williams,' Bill said. 'But

then you already knew that. I saw you at my trial, making notes.'

'The duties of a newspaper man, I'm afraid.'

Bill frowned and then, in order to get the conversation back on track, continued, 'So who would I send with my letter? A good rider, you said. Do you know of such a man?'

The small man smiled. 'I'll deliver your letter myself,' he said.

'You? A newspaper man?'

'I'm also an expert rider,' the man said. 'I rode for the pony express in my youth, which was how I got into this business in the first place. The pony express, the telegraph system and the newspaper business are all much the same. They're all about the distribution of information.'

'I'd certainly like my information distributed.'

I'll take the letter for you.'

'You'd do that?'

'I will.'

Bill hadn't expected this and the turn

of events threw him into a bit of a quandary. But he felt he was a good judge of character and all his instincts were telling him he could trust the small man. The man was built like a jockey and if he could handle a horse the way he claimed, then he would certainly make good speed.

'Then I accept your offer of assistance,' Bill said. 'Maybe this town isn't so rotten after all.'

'Well, mister,' the small man said, 'if you really think you have a chance to go against the Stantons and can prove it to the town, then you'll find no shortage of men willing to help. Lots of folk in town would go up against the Stantons if there was someone to show them the way. Living in fear ain't healthy for a man, nor is paying the insurances the Stantons demand of us.'

'So let me get this clear,' Bill said. 'You want to ride out of here and deliver my letter?'

'Indeed I do and will.'

'You mean that?'

'I do,' the man nodded. 'Come on. Let's write out your letter and I'll tell you about it.'

'That's bloody marvellous,' Bill said. He grinned and followed the small man through to the back of the building.

8

They had decided Bill would not attempt to break the kid out of the jail until after Thomson had ridden out of town and yet a further hour had gone by. If things went wrong with the jailbreak then at least Thomson would be well on his way to Fort Hood, and before anyone knew the newspaperman had gone he would be too far away to stop. This had been Thomson's idea, and although Bill had no doubt that the jailbreak would prove successful, he had to admit it made perfect sense to be cautious.

They had also roped in another man, or rather Thomson had, when he had taken Bill across the moonlit street towards the livery stable. Bill had been cautious as they crossed the street, his hands hovering over his Colts but they made the journey without incident.

Once inside the stable Thomson had roused the owner, finding him asleep, covered in a filthy horse blanket, in one corner of the stable. An elderly man with so much beard that it was impossible to put an age upon him. He could have been in his sixties, seventies or even eighties. The way he walked, with his back all stooped up suggested he was ancient but his eyes shone with the vitality of youth. The old man had but the one tooth in his head, dead centre it hung down like a gleaming tusk. His name was Sam and the newspaperman knew him well, told Bill they had been friends for a great many years.

Bill had stood aside, watching the exchange between the two men with some amusement. As soon as the newspaperman outlined the plan to break the kid free and then notify the US marshal, Sam had become particularly animated. He had cursed the entire Stanton clan, said it was not before time that someone around here had the gumption to go up against them. The old man had looked Bill up and down for several moments and, looking unimpressed, had gone and saddled Thomson's horse.

And now Thomson had gone and Bill placed his knitting into his saddle-bags and looked at the old man.

'Have you got it now?' he asked.

'Sure,' the old man snapped and bit off a chunk of chewing tobacco, which was a considerable feat given that he had but the single tooth. He pressed the tobacco plug against his lower gum and bit down. 'You told me a half dozen times and I heard you the first as well as the last.'

'Better to make certain, *boyo*.'

The old man smiled, once again revealing his tooth. 'I sure do hope you know what you're doing,' he said.

'I've faced greater odds than an old man and his offspring,' Bill said and then went off on one of his familiar tangents. 'Did I tell you I was at the Little Bighorn?'

'You didn't.'

'Well I was. And I'm still here.'

'There were no survivors of the Little Bighorn,' the old man said, grinning. This Welshman sure was a one for these fish tales.

'That's what they say,' Bill agreed.

The old man looked at Bill, unsure what to make of this man.

'Well come on then,' Bill said, presently. 'Let's go and wake the sheriff.'

Once again Bill found himself crossing Main Street. It was now several hours beyond midnight and the entire town had fallen silent. He walked, the old man beside him, with great caution. His hands swung casually at his sides but this belied the fact that he was ready to go for his guns in a second should the need arise. Thankfully there was no such need and they reached the jailhouse without incident.

'You get the man out here,' Bill said and stood to the side of the door, his back against the wall and a Colt in hand. He wasn't at all sure he'd be able to pull the same trick on the sheriff that he'd used on the newspaperman. The sheriff's deputies would surely have been missed by now, which would have at least put the sheriff on guard.

The old man nodded and walked up to the heavy door. He was just about to rap upon it when he had an idea. He reached out and grasped the door handle, twisted it gently and sure enough the door swung open.

The old man looked at Bill, shrugged his shoulders.

'Guess the sheriff feels safe enough not to lock the door,' the old man whispered.

'Bloody marvellous,' Bill said and quietly stepped into the jailhouse. He motioned for the old man to follow and then gently closed the door behind them. They stood there for a moment while their eyes grew acclimatized to the gloom. They could hear snoring, the sheriff most likely, coming from the back of the building.

'Looks like we caught him napping,' Bill whispered.

The two men moved through the jailhouse, heading towards the rear of the building where the sheriff's snoring seem to be originating from. They froze when the old man bumped against the side of a desk. The muffled retort sounded to both men like thunder.

'Be careful,' Bill whispered.

'Can't see a darn thing,' the old man grumbled back.

'Well get behind me,' Bill said. 'Shadow my steps.'

'Need some light to make a shadow,' the old man grumbled and fell in directly behind the Welshman.

They made the back of the room without further incident and were presented with another door. Bill opened it, lifting the handle as he pushed inwards. The door creaked once but only briefly and Bill and the old man stepped through it to find the sleeping form of the sheriff. Bill looked around and through the dimness he could see the doorway that led through to the cells, where only yesterday he had been nursing a battered head.

So much had happened since then.

Two men had died since then.

The sheriff had constructed a hammock in the corner of the office and somehow had gotten his bulk into it. It was secured to a beam at one end and to a hook that had been driven into the wall at the other. The canvas strained with the lawman's considerable weight.

The sheriff, unaware of his two visitors, slept soundly.

Bill pointed to a shotgun that was leaning against the wall. The old man understood the gesture and went and got the rifle. Bill took a look around, peering into the darkness, and noticed the sheriff wasn't wearing his gun-belt. The old man spotted it hanging on a nail in the wall behind the sheriff. He pointed it out to Bill and then carefully went and took it down.

The sheriff was unarmed and now had no chance of getting to his weapons.

This was good because Bill didn't want any shooting if he could help it. The sound of gunfire would bring too many people running.

'Stand back,' Bill said to the old man and then brought a leg up under the hammock and kicked out, toppling it. The sheriff came awake instantly, his eyes snapping open, startled, confused. Bill kicked again, sending the lawman falling to the floor with a dull thud, which drove all the wind from his body.

'Really shouldn't sleep on the job, Sheriff,' Bill said, pointing his Colt directly at the lawman's head. 'Now get up.'

The sheriff was unable to immediately oblige. All the wind had been driven from his body in the fall and he struggled to catch his breath. Added to that he was a big man who didn't find it easy getting to his feet at the best of times.

'What's happening out there?' The kid's voice came from behind the large door that led to the cells. There was fear in his tone. He was probably thinking the noise meant a lynch mob arranged by Stanton had come for him.

'Quiet, kid,' Bill answered. 'We'll have you out of there in a moment.'

'Bill? Is that you?'

'It's me, kid. Now quit jawing,' Bill said and looked back down at the lawman. 'Now get that lard-arse up.'

'Come on, fat man,' the old man said, clearly relishing the situation. 'You can move quicker than that. I've seen you jump when Stanton calls.'

The sheriff had recovered enough to take stock of the situation and he looked up at the two men holding weapons on him.

'Where's my men?' he asked.

'You mean your deputies,' Bill said. 'They won't be gunning anyone down anytime soon. Now I won't tell you again. Get up.'

Awkwardly the sheriff managed to get to his feet. He stood there, panting, spittle in the corner of his mouth, and looked directly at the old man. He was unaware of how ridiculous he looked standing there in his underwear.

'You're making a big mistake, Sam,' he said. It was obviously meant as a threat but the sheriff didn't seem to be in any position to threaten anyone at the moment.

'Shut up,' Bill snapped. 'Get the keys. Release the kid.'

'What are you planning to do?'

'Get the keys,' Bill insisted and prodded the sheriff's fat belly with the eye of his Colt.

The sheriff stood his ground. 'Where are my deputies?' he asked.

'They're dead,' Bill said. 'And unless you want to be joining them you'd better spring the kid.'

'You won't get away with this,' the sheriff said and again cast a glance at the old man. 'You can't go around killing officers of the law. You'll swing for this. Both of you.'

'They intended on killing me,' Bill snapped back. 'Law ain't supposed to go around killing people.'

'You won't get away with this,' the sheriff insisted.

'I will not tell you again, *boyo*,' Bill said and levelled the Colt so that it pointed directly between the lawman's eyes.

His finger tensed on the trigger.

The sheriff went to his desk and took the set of heavy keys from his drawer.

9

'So what happens now?' the old man asked. The kid was free, the sheriff was slumped in his chair, looking like the sorriest critter that ever walked the earth, and it suddenly occurred to the old man that he didn't have the faintest idea where they were going to go from there. He knew some sort of line had been crossed but he wasn't at all sure what that meant.

'What time do you figure it is?' Bill asked and then noticed the sheriff's chain hanging from his waistcoat. He pushed the barrel of the Colt beneath the chain and lifted, pulling the lawman's timepiece from his pocket. 'Three. Figure we've maybe a hour or two before dawn.'

'You're all going to hang for this,' the sheriff said and looked at the old man who was holding the shotgun aimed square at his stomach.

'You best start riding, Sheriff,' Bill said.

Neither the old man nor the kid said anything, but they both shot questions at Bill with their eyes. Bill smiled at them and then bent menacingly towards the sheriff and when the lawman cowered in his chair, Bill reached out and snatched the badge from his waistcoat.

'You ain't entitled to wear this,' he said, turning it over and over in his hand. He looked back at the sheriff and when he next spoke there was grit in his voice. 'I want you to ride out to your boss.'

'I ain't got no boss,' the sheriff snapped back. This earned him a snort of derision from both the old man and the kid.

'Your boss,' Bill continued, 'Old Man Stanton, you tell him that we've taken the town back. He's no longer running things around here.' Bill paused; a thoughtful look crossed his face. He tossed the sheriff's badge to the old man. 'You tell him that Sam here is the new law in town. You tell him the kid and myself are his deputies.'

'You're crazy,' the now ex-sheriff said. 'He's nothing but a broken down old man.'

The new sheriff came forward and for a moment it looked as if he was going to bring the butt of the shotgun into his predecessor's face, show the fat man just how broken down he was. But then he smiled and pinned the badge to his shirt.

'Better a broken down old man,' he said, 'than a corrupt tub of lard.'

'My sentiments exactly,' Bill said and then quickly added: 'Not that I'm saying you're broken down, mind.'

'You have been booted out of office, Sheriff Clemens,' the kid said, grinning.

'Ain't no Sheriff Clemens about it. He's no longer the sheriff,' the old man said, proudly pushing his chest forward to show his badge. 'From now on he's simply Fats Clemens.'

'Good a name as any,' Bill said. 'Now come on, Fats. Get going and tell Stanton if he wants trouble, best leave it till gone noon. I'd like to get a little shut-eye.'

The sheriff, or rather ex-sheriff, got to his feet slowly as if unsure of himself and fearing one or other of the men was going to open fire at any moment. This didn't make any kind of sense to him. The logical thing to do after springing the kid would be to vamoose, try to get as far away as possible before the shooting started, but this Welshman was anything but logical. He'd broken into the jailhouse in the dead of night, well walked in, calm as you like, and now he seemed to be intent on hanging around and facing the might of the Stantons. On the face of it he would have no chance, but Clemens didn't think it wise to underestimate the man. He had already somehow bested two well-armed deputies without so much as a pocketknife in his possession. He'd been unarmed when the deputies had escorted him out of Stanton but somehow he'd gotten the better of them.

'You're letting me ride away?' Clemens, the onetime lawman, asked.

'No,' Bill said, smiling. 'I'm sending you on an errand. You tell Stanton all I've said and also inform him that if he comes looking for trouble I'll send him straight to hell.'

Clemens didn't answer, merely stared at Bill for a moment. There was something in the Welshman's eyes that told the fat man his words, as incredible as they sounded, were no idle boasts. And for the first time in many years, the man considered the possibility that Stanton, for all the muscle he commanded, all the guns at his disposal, may not be indestructible after all.

'Now get going,' Bill said. 'Before I change my mind and gun you down here and now. We could hold a trial, say you attacked the new sheriff and I, like a good deputy, sprung to his defence.'

Clemens shook his head.

'You ain't going to get away with this,' he said once more and started towards the front of the jailhouse. His steps were slow and Bill helped him on his way with a well-aimed boot to his backside. That provoked a whoop of delight from the new sheriff.

Once outside Bill ordered the old man and the kid to stay in the jailhouse while he escorted Clemens to his horse and set him on his way. Neither of the men was happy with this, but when they protested Bill cut them short, telling them he would be back in few moments and explain what had to be done. He didn't elaborate on that and once again crossed the silent street, this time with the redundant lawman walking before him.

They made their way to the livery stable where Clemens's horse was housed in a reserved stall. The night was starting to give way to the day and in little more than an hour it would be dawn. Bill wanted to get the fat man well on his way before first light.

'What are you trying to achieve here?' Clemens asked, presently as he pulled his horse from its stall. He located his saddle in its usual place and threw it on to the horse. Next he bent to secure the straps and then turned back to Bill, who had kept his Colt trained on him throughout the entire operation. 'Well?' he prompted.

Bill looked back at the man, said nothing.

'Hell,' Clemens said. 'I knew you was loco the first time I met you. Just didn't figure out just how loco you truly were.'

Again Bill said nothing and gestured with the Colt for Clemens to mount up, which the man did with surprising agility for someone so big.

'My guns?' Clemens asked, hopefully.

'I think we'll hang on to them,' Bill said, smiling. 'Seems the wise thing to do. And besides who would want to shoot you?'

For a moment there was silence between the two men. It was Clemens who finally spoke.

'I'll just ride out of here then,' he said, sat astride the horse, eyes scanning the Welshman. It was obvious he was still unable to believe what was happening, and was fully expecting to be gunned down at any moment.

'Bloody marvellous,' Bill said, smiling. He walked behind Clemens as the man rode out of the livery stable and on to the street. Bill remained there for some time, watching Clemens ride out of town, all the while wondering what train of events this latest escapade had set into motion.

Still, he reasoned, whatever happened next would not be his fault. He was the one who had been transgressed against. It was he who had been dragged before a kangaroo court in which all due process was ignored. And if things had gone the way Stanton had planned then he would, at this very moment, be lying in a shallow grave.

Too much had happened for him to simply ride away and as his da, had always said, '*Chorddi 'r arall boch boyo a cei daro ail*,' which roughly translated as, 'You turn the other cheek, *boyo* and you get smacked again.'

10

'He said what?' Abaddon Stanton snarled.

He couldn't believe what he was hearing and the news, brought by the sheriff, had made him furious. Sheriff — that was a joke, since Clemens claimed that rickety old man from the livery stable had now assumed the responsibilities of town sheriff. And it got worse — that infernal Welshman, who seemed to be behind this, and Henry Carthy were acting as deputies.

It seemed the Welshman had just ridden back into town, presumably after killing the two heavily armed deputies who had been ordered to kill him and somehow turning the tables and beating the two men. And if that wasn't enough, he had proceeded to bust the kid out of jail and then run the sheriff out of town, but only after removing his badge of office and appointing the livery man as Clemens's replacement.

Abaddon would have none of this. This was his town; this town carried his name. And he vowed that before the day was out the Welshman would be on the ground begging, grovelling at his feet.

'You have proven yourself useless,' Abaddon said, turning to the fat man who had only hours ago been town sheriff. 'You're no good to me. You don't deserve to be sheriff. You are incompetent, and worse, a coward.'

Clemens said nothing and watched as the old man's hotheaded grandson, Caleb, crossed between them and stood before the fire. It was he who had started all this. It was he who had done something untoward, whatever the hell that was, to the kid's mother and provoked this entire mess. Until the kid had bust into the saloon intent on killing Cal Stanton, the Welshman had been content to play cards. If Cal hadn't started all this then maybe they would never have heard the name, William Williams. The Welshman would have ridden on, taken his funny ways with him, and life would have gone on pretty much as it always had.

Instead they had all this.

'Useless,' Abaddon muttered, more to himself than anyone else and sank wearily into the chair beside the large fireplace. His eyes stared into the flames as he breathed deeply to regain his composure. What was there to be done about the accursed Welshman?

'I'll ride into town now,' Caleb said. 'Take a couple of men with me and kill that Welshman stone dead.'

'That's precisely what you will not do,' Abaddon answered, sharply. The old man didn't so much as look at his grandson, and instead continued to gaze into the dancing flames of the fire.

Caleb glared at his grandfather for a moment before speaking. The old man was aware of that stare, he felt it, knew that the look in his grandson's eyes was not one of family loyalty but of resentment, and maybe even the seeds of hate.

'You let this Welshman get away with this,' Caleb warned, 'and pretty soon you'll lose control of the town. That's if you've not already lost control. These men who your court convicted are walking around as free as the day they were born. Something must be done about this and done immediately.'

'I am well aware of what must be done,' Abaddon said. 'And I also know the way it must be done.'

For several moments there was silence, while the old man continued to stare deep into the fire as if consulting some oracle within its flames and seeking wisdom therein. Caleb and the ousted sheriff simply stood there, saying nothing but both privately thinking up a storm.

'I'll take a ride into town immediately following breakfast,' Abaddon said. 'Take a couple of men with me and see if we can't reason with this Welshman.'

'He won't listen to any talk,' Caleb

said. 'Your court already ordered him out of town, never to return. Look at the contempt he has for that ruling. There is only one language men like this understand and that is the word of the gun.'

Abaddon turned from the fire and stood to his full height. He glared at his grandson and momentarily the years seemed to fall from him. Where only seconds ago he had seemed a frail old man, someone in the final stages of his life, he now seemed young, virile and strong.

'At times I despair of you,' the old man said. He had loved his late daughter, the boy's mother, with all his heart. Not a day went by that he didn't miss her. Indeed he often lay awake at night, remembering the warmth of her smile and the softness of her embrace, but, and not for the first time, he cursed her memory for giving him a grandson like Caleb. The boy's father had been killed in an Indian attack and his mother had never remarried, had given all her attention to her son. Caleb had been spoilt all his life and now he was a hothead and an idiot. They had indulged him too much over the years, answered his every whim. When he had gotten in trouble they had been there to ensure the consequences were not too great. It had made him arrogant to the point of recklessness.

'You will remain here,' the old man said. 'You have caused quite enough trouble.'

'I'm riding in with you,' Caleb protested.

'You will remain here,' Abaddon said. 'And that is final.'

Caleb said nothing but his look spoke volumes.

11

'Right,' Bill said, climbing up on to the stool. 'Let's be having your full attention, please.'

He looked around the saloon and supposed that, all things considered, given the hold the Stantons had on the town, this was quite a healthy gathering. There were maybe fifty of the town's citizens crowded into the saloon.

'I'm pleased you could all come,' he said. He was aware that the town's people, or at least those present, were unsure of what was going on and, far from wanting to fight for their town, were only there out of curiosity. When the bullets started flying the greatest majority of them would have taken flight before the smell of cordite settled on the air. He caught Sam's eyes and gave him a slight smile. The old man had certainly whipped up a crowd, running around town, proudly wearing his new sheriff's badge, and calling an extraordinary town meeting.

'By now you are all aware of what has happened during the night,' Bill said and noticed all eyes momentarily turn to the old man and the kid. 'You all went to bed last night under a cloud of tyranny, but you have awoken to a new day and a new town. You have a new sheriff; no longer is an innocent young man waiting in your jailhouse for an unjust hanging. This town is now your town.'

That received a light applause.

'You, as free citizens of this town have a duty to stand by your new sheriff. You must all stand firm and fend off the evil that would attempt to force its will upon you.'

The crowd were held rapt by Bill's speech and the Welshman smiled inwardly. As he spoke he was thinking of his late *da*, of the speeches he had watched him give to the Miner's Association gatherings back in the old country. This current situation reminded Bill of the struggles back home. Stanton, with his iron grip on the town, was not a million miles away from the mine owners who had sought to keep the workforce in its place. Their tactics were of intimidation and attrition, and were not that far removed from the methods Stanton used to maintain his control over the town.

Bill had decided he would keep the news that Thomson, the newspaperman was currently riding for help, a secret unless it became absolutely necessary to share the information. He didn't want Stanton getting wind of it and sending out men to stop Thomson. There was little chance anyone would be able to catch up with the newspaperman — he would have made good distance by now — but it seemed prudent to keep quiet on this point, at least until the man's absence was noticed.

'No doubt Stanton and his men will make an appearance in town today,' Bill said. 'But your sheriff here will stand against them and we, his deputies will be beside him. It is hoped that many of you will support us. For to back down to Stanton now means that this town, your homes, will never truly belong to you and neither will your hearts. Freedom comes at a price and it is a price you will all ultimately have to pay.' And that, Bill thought, was bloody poetry.

Poetic or not, the speech was met with a stony silence, which was finally broken by a woman, small child in arms, who had pushed her way to the front of the crowd.

'You speak well,' she said and Bill, who had always been proud of his oratorical skills, smiled. 'But your words, no matter how pretty, will not make our men bullet-proof.'

'Martha,' a bearded man shouted from the rear of the room as he climbed on to a table to get a better view of the woman. 'This is a saloon, my wife. No place for a woman. Go home and take our child with you. Leave this to the men folk.'

'Go boil your head,' came the woman's reply, which provoked laughter from the gathered crowd.

The new sheriff, who was obviously very much of the old school, glared at the woman.

'You disrespect your man,' he said.

'And I'll disrespect you, you old coot,' the woman retorted and once again her words received a wave of laughter.

The sheriff didn't seem to know what to do. From the look on his face it seemed the woman was about to become his first arrest. He brushed a hand over his badge as if to draw attention to his authority and glared at the woman.

'Those of you who wish to join the fight and can handle a firearm will be most welcome,' Bill said, grinning despite the gravity of the situation. 'All we ask of anyone else is that you stay out of harm's way until this works itself out. I believe that the Stantons operate on the assumption that no one will dare to go against them. If the town stands together then I do not believe it will come to a fight. I do not think the Stantons have the stomach for a real fight. It is one thing to push men about when you come in force, but quite another thing to stand against equal numbers.'

'That's brave talk for a newcomer,' the woman said and shifted the baby in her arms. 'You do not know the situation around here, nor do you know the Stantons. What does this town matter to you? You have no roots here and you will be gone soon enough.'

This time the woman's husband didn't intervene and what's more her latest outburst elicited murmurs of agreement rather than laughter from the crowd.

'What is it you all want?' Henry yelled, lifting himself up and sitting on the long counter that ran the length of the saloon. 'Do any of you enjoy paying the town tax to the Stantons? Do any of you think I deserved to hang for challenging Caleb Stanton? Do any of you think my trial was legal? The sentence not already decided before even one word was uttered in my defence? I'm not afraid of the Stantons and I will stand beside this man,' he pointed towards Bill. 'And what's more I shall be proud to do so.'

An almost imperceptible applause.

'Whatever happens,' Bill said, knowing that he was losing control of the meeting, that the agenda was heading in a direction he hadn't planned for, 'it's as simple as this. I am not going away until the Stanton problem is over. It is true this is not my town but the Stantons have wronged me. Only yesterday I had to kill two men, deputies of this town, nonetheless, who had been ordered to kill me. Shoot me in the back, most likely.

'I do not enjoy killing but what's been done cannot be undone and, like it or not, this town is heading for a showdown between myself, those who stand besides me and the Stantons.

Being in the crossfire would be dangerous and that's all I want to say.'

'So what do we do now?' asked a man, whom Bill recognized as Dutch Carter, one of the men he had been playing poker with that afternoon when this all started. It seemed like a million years ago now.

'Go about your business as usual,' Bill said. 'But when Stanton turns up either get behind me or get hidden.'

'I'll be with you,' Dutch Carter said and a few people murmured in agreement.

'Good,' Bill said. 'And I'm pleased to have you.' He could see it in the eyes of the people gathered that many of them would have liked to make a stand against the Stantons, but a pragmatism born of fear stopped them from stepping forward. He could understand that, but he knew from experience that one day a person had to face up to that which oppresses them.

12

Incredibly, with the threat hanging over the town, the likelihood of extreme violence at any moment, the people went about their day-to-day business. The saloon was opened at 10 a.m. as usual, the school took in its students and the general store, bank and hotel were all trading. The main street, as always, was a hive of activity and to the casual onlooker it would seem that all was as it should be in the small town, but anyone attuned in such a way would have detected the hint of trepidation in the air, noted the look of fear in the eyes of the citizens.

Bill was sat in the sheriff's office, knitting, while he waited for the inevitable. He had expected the Stantons to have already arrived in force, but as it fast approached noon all was quiet. The new sheriff sat dozing behind his desk, his feet up on the finely polished surface and his tattered hat pulled down over his eyes. Only Henry seemed tense and for the last hour, had been pacing the room. Twice he had twirled on his feet and pulled iron to practise his draw. The Welshman found this very distracting as he tried to work on the horse blanket.

'Why don't you go and get some rest,' Bill said and skilfully closed another stitch, knotting the wool.

'I'm staying with you,' the kid retorted and continued with his pacing.

'Bloody marvellous,' Bill said and went back to his knitting.

Moments later Dutch Carter, who had elected himself lookout man, came tearing down the main street on his cayuse pony. He pulled the horse to a dead stop outside the jailhouse and positively leapt from the saddle. For a moment his feet did a comical jig but somehow he managed to remain on his feet and not fall arse over elbow into the dirt.

'Stanton's coming,' he yelled as he

burst through the doors and into the jailhouse, waking the old man and causing the kid to draw iron.

'Put that away,' Bill said to the kid as he calmly and carefully placed his knitting into his saddle-bags. 'Right then,' he said, finally. 'No doubt a merry dance awaits us.'

'I won't be dancing,' the kid said. 'I'll be shooting.'

'As useful a musical accompaniment as any for the tune we have in mind,' Bill said and walked out on to the street. He no longer carried the rifle in the pouch behind his back, but he still wore the twin Colts low on his hips.

The street was as it had been only moments ago with no sign of any of the Stanton clan.

'There,' Dutch said, pointing to the far end of the street and sure enough the unmistakable form of Abaddon Stanton came into view followed by three other riders. People crossed the street quickly as they sought cover.

From this distance Bill couldn't put a

face to any of the men, with the exception of Abaddon who was unmistakable in his black frock coat and white Stetson, but the rider bringing up the rear looked to be the short, stocky man who had aided Caleb Stanton in giving the kid such a beating in the saloon. Bill frowned. He had expected a bigger show of force than this and he wondered if Stanton had men placed all around them, keeping themselves out of sight until they were called upon. Did gunmen in Stanton's employ already surround them? Were gun-sights already trained upon them?

The Welshman stood there, the other three men bunched up closely behind him.

'You gonna handle this, Sheriff?' Bill said with more than a hint of black humour in his voice.

'I sure am,' the old man said and pushed forward to stand besides Bill. He ignored the looks Dutch and Henry shot at him. 'You gonna aid me, Deputy?'

'I sure am,' Bill said, smiling.

'We're all in this,' the kid said and

then looked at Dutch. 'Ain't that right?'

'Sure is,' Dutch said, though he didn't sound too sure of himself.

Bill knew that the three men, with the possible exception of the kid, who was hotheaded enough to face the hounds of hell, were relying on him to take the lead. He was the one who had whipped them up, and it sure wouldn't do for him to lose his resolve just yet. He had started the wheel spinning and it had to follow its inevitable course, even if that course did lead to bloodshed.

'Don't anyone get jumpy and pull iron,' Bill said, directing his words at the kid more than to any of the others. 'Stanton may consider this his town, but it's unlikely he'll want to shoot us down in broad daylight with so many witnesses. My guess is that before there's any lead flying, Old Man Stanton will be nowhere in the vicinity.'

'If they don't want to fight then why are they here?' the kid asked.

'Likely to assess the situation,' Bill

said. 'All they know is what Clemens would have told them. The fact that the old man's leading them suggests this ain't gonna become a gunfight.'

'Sure would be a good time for your cavalry to arrive,' the sheriff said and Bill shot him a glance.

'We keep that to ourselves for the moment,' he said. 'Let's just see what Stanton has to say for himself.' It was extremely unlikely now that anyone would be able to catch up with Thomson, and by first light tomorrow, if not sooner, the newspaperman would have reached Fort Hood.

'What cavalry?' the kid asked, and Dutch echoed the question with his eyes.

Bill looked at the kid and smiled. 'Must have forgot to mention it,' he said. 'Let's just say I've stacked the hand in our favour, but I'd like to keep that particular ace up my sleeve for the moment.'

Dutch breathed a sigh of relief and all of a sudden he seemed to grow ten feet.

'Let's show them they ain't running

this town no more,' he said.

'Bloody marvellous,' Bill said, and now that the riders were close enough, he made eye contact with the man who had presided over the shambles of a trial. The man who had, in one way or another, sentenced both Bill and the kid to death. If things had gone the old man's way they would both be dead now, and yet they were both standing here, ready to face him down. That must really be sticking in the old bastard's craw.

The four riders, Abaddon in the lead, stopped their horses a few feet from the men outside the jailhouse. Abaddon looked each of the men over in turn and then smiled.

'What's going on here?' he asked. 'And why is that old fool wearing the badge of law?'

'Ain't no fool about it,' Sam said and held Abaddon's gaze. 'I'm the new law in these parts.'

This provoked laughter from the three men with Abaddon, but the old man himself didn't even blink. He

97

glared at the man wearing the badge and then his eyes locked on Bill.

'You instigated all this,' he said. It wasn't a question.

'No,' Bill shook his head. 'You did. You charged me with being a vagrant, took my money and ran me out of town. Those deputies you sent to escort me — to kill me — their blood is also on your hands. It was you that started all this off and the only way it's gonna end is with you gone or in the ground.'

For a moment a look of pure fury crossed Abaddon's face but then he simply smiled and shook his head.

'I did nothing but my duty under law,' the old man said.

'*Celwyddwr, celwyddwr 'ch re bum acha danio,*' Bill said and didn't bother translating the insult, feeling its meaning would be conveyed by the tone of his voice.

'We're going to ride out of here today,' Abaddon said with a frown. 'And if, when we return, you and these three fools have left town then that will be the end of it. If you're still here, then I shall be forced to remove you.'

Bill stepped forward and allowed a hand to brush the heel of one of his Colts. 'Like your fat sheriff, you've already been removed, and are in no position to make demands,' he snapped back. 'This town no longer answers to you.'

'You're a big man with those guns,' the man Bill recognized as the squat man who had been with Caleb Stanton, said. As he had been then, he appeared to be unarmed. He simply sat there upon his horse, staring at Bill.

'I don't need my guns to whip a fool like you,' Bill said. 'Back home I fought bigger and better.'

'You don't want to be doing that,' the sheriff said, grabbing Bill by the arm. 'He used to box for the army; he's killed men with his bare hands. He's got a head like a rock and fists like hammers.'

'Don't look much to me,' Bill said and reached down and unhooked his gun-belt. He handed it to the sheriff and noticed the smile cross Abaddon's face when he did so. Once again he wondered if there were gunmen stationed around town, but he put the thought out of his mind. It was more likely that Stanton didn't think anyone would be able to best his man in a fistfight. Well, once again, Bill was going to show him how wrong he was.

The squat man jumped from his horse and the beast seemed to sigh its relief as the weight was removed from its back.

'You're a darn fool, Welshman,' the sheriff said. 'But I sure do admire your grit.'

Bill smiled and then looked at the remaining riders before turning to the kid.

'Hold your fire,' he said. 'If any of these gentlemen so much as twitch you blow Stanton away. Otherwise hold your fire while I teach this fool here a lesson,' he pointed to indicate the squat man who had removed his shirt and was now ready for a fight.

'You gonna fight or you gonna talk?' the squat man prompted.

'Oh, I'm most certainly gonna fight you,' Bill said and smiled. 'But just give me a moment.' He looked at Old Man Stanton. He was sat upon his horse, a grin plastered across his ugly face. 'You tell your men to hold their fire.'

Stanton nodded.

'You have my word,' he said.

'Bloody marvellous,' Bill said and once more turned to the kid. 'Now do as I say and hold your fire. Do not shoot unless any of these men make a move to do so.' He indicated to Stanton and the riders.

'What if he beats you?' the kid asked.

'That ain't bloody likely,' Bill said and stepped out into the street. 'I used to box for Glamorgan when I was a schoolboy.'

'The kid nodded, said nothing.

'Gentlemen, give us room,' Bill said and removed his shirt, stripping down to his vest.

13

It suddenly occurred to Bill that he didn't even know the squat man's name. Here he was, about to engage in the ancient gentlemanly endeavour of boxing, and he didn't know the name of his opponent.

Bill spat on the palms of his hands and then rubbed them together. He hopped up and down a little and then took two quick swipes at thin air, leading with his right hand. He then danced a little more, his upper body rocking gently with his legs seeming independent to the rest of him.

'What's your name?' he asked.

The squat man was watching Bill in astonishment. During all his years' boxing for the army, and in all the fights since, he had never seen a fighter dance in quite the same way as this Welshman.

'My name?' he looked at Bill.

'I take it you have one.'

'I have a name.'

'Then what is it?'

'What do you want to know it for?'

'Well,' Bill said and without warning moved forward, connecting a stinging left hook to the other man's jaw, taking him off his feet. 'It would be nice to know who I'm fighting.'

The effect of Bill's blow was all but momentary, and the squat man shook off the surprise and leapt back to his feet.

'Bear,' he screamed. 'They call me Bear.'

'No doubt named after your mother,' Bill said and danced some more.

Bear lunged at Bill, keeping his head down and his arms upright, trying to use his own body as a battering ram, but the Welshman skilfully sidestepped him and delivered a chop to the back of the man's neck.

'Pleased to be of your acquaintance, Bear,' Bill said and hopped from one leg to the other. He noticed the sheriff leaning forward in delight, his single tooth gleaming in the cavern that was his open mouth. The kid, too, looked pleased at this turn of events, amused even.

Bill cast a quick glance at Stanton and saw the look of anger on the old man's face; the veins in his forehead looked fit to burst at any moment and his face had gone two shades of red. A crowd had gathered in the street and even though they kept their distance, they were no longer hiding away from the Stantons.

Bill was quite pleased with that.

Bear rolled about on the ground and screamed out in fury. He scooped up a handful of dirt and thrust it into Bill's face.

Momentarily blinded, the Welshman stumbled backwards, his hands rubbing the dirt from his watering eyes. That was all his opponent needed and Bear got to his feet and delivered a punishing blow to Bill's stomach, doubling the Welshman over. He followed up by bringing his knee up into the Welshman's chin. The blow crunched Bill's jaw together and set off bells ringing inside his head.

And then it was Bill's turn to hit the ground.

Bear wasn't going to fight cleanly, then, which wasn't that much of a surprise to the Welshman and he cursed himself for losing his concentration and allowing the other man to gain the advantage. That stupid mistake was going to cost him heavy, Bill realized, as Bear bent over him and hammered a left into his face.

Bill knew that he had to get out of this or he was finished. His head was pounding and he tasted blood on the back of his tongue. He tried to roll and unbalance the other man, but Bear simply bent over and grabbed him by the neck, snaking his podgy fingers around the Welshman's throat and starting to squeeze.

Bill gritted his teeth and with all his might brought his leg up, a knee connected with Bear's groin. Bill hadn't been able to muster that much force into the blow, but in such a sensitive area it was enough and Bear groaned, loosened his grip on Bill's throat and fell over sideways.

It was the chance the Welshman needed and Bill sprung to his feet. He squeezed his eyes closed and rubbed them once again. His vision was all to hell but he could, at least, see his opponent.

Bear got awkwardly to his feet, and Bill immediately put him back down again with a combination of blows to the head.

Bill took the opportunity to step back several paces while Bear recovered and used the time to clear his eyes of the stinging dirt and grit. Bill noticed old man Stanton shift uneasily upon his horse as he looked at his man, still sprawled in the dirt. It would be clear to the old man now that the outcome of the fight was not a certain thing. Once again he had underestimated the Welshman.

'He getting up?' Bill asked, smearing

a trickle of blood from the corner of his mouth. 'Or is he finished?'

'I'm gonna kill you,' Bear said as he looked up at Bill and tried to get to his feet, but all he could manage was to get to his knees. He knelt there, panting like a dog while blood gushed from his smashed mouth.

He spat out several of his teeth.

'Finish him off,' the kid yelled.

'Never hit a man when he's down,' Bill said. 'That's not the way we do it.'

Bear, though, had no such sense of fair play, and he used the opportunity when the Welshman was distracted to suddenly leap to his feet and charge him. Once more he tried to use his body as a battering ram but Bill, who saw him at the last moment, was too quick and easily stepped aside and brought his boot into Bear's backside to help him along. Once again Bear hit the ground, face first, eating dirt, only this time he didn't seem to want to get back up.

'I think he's finished himself off,' Bill said.

Only Bear wasn't finished. Not by a long shot and once again he managed to find his feet. He snarled like a wild animal and again charged, but there was no grace in his movement, and Bill was once more easily able to step aside. The Welshman stretched out a foot, tripping Bear and sending him back to the ground.

'Stay down,' Bill said and moved in closer to the fallen man. 'Stay down and I won't have to hit you again.'

Bear yelled something unintelligible and pushed himself back to his feet but the Welshman was too quick and a combination of blows finally finished him off. Bear's eyes rolled back in his head, his legs buckled beneath him and he fell back to the ground, unconscious.

'Stop this, stop this,' Old Man Stanton yelled, and then a look of sheer agony crossed his face. He gave a guttural groan, pitched forward in his saddle and hit the ground hard.

14

'It's his heart,' Doc Curtis said.

Bill looked at the sawbones and then at the figure of the old man in the bed. He looked so frail, a harmless old man. Was this really the man who had held the town in an iron grip for so many years?

'Is he going to live?' he asked.

The doc took a long look at his patient before answering. 'Too soon to tell,' he said. 'He's alive for now, at least.'

Immediately after he had collapsed, Bill, Dutch, Henry and Stanton's men — well, the two that could still stand at least — had carried the old man over to the town's hotel where a bed was immediately found for him on the ground floor, and the doctor sent for. The kid couldn't see the point in all this, didn't understand why they didn't just let the old man die in the street, but as soon as he voiced these thoughts he was stopped dead by a look from Bill.

'He needs rest now,' the doctor said. 'I'll look back in on him in an hour but for now he should be left alone. There are far too many people in this room. One of you should stay with him, but the rest of you had best leave.'

'I ain't leaving Mr Stanton alone,' said Jake Tanner. He was one of the men who had ridden in with the old man. His pard stood next to him and nodded in agreement.

Bill looked at the two men, and despite the fact that they were to all intents and purposes, the enemy, he had to admire their loyalty to their boss.

'There ain't nothing you two can do for him,' he said. 'You'd be better off taking care of Bear.'

'I ain't leaving,' Jake insisted and the tension seemed to grow inside the room. The man left his arms hanging, ready to draw should the need arise. 'I

110

ain't leaving Mr Stanton to you varmints.'

'What do you think we'll do to him?' Bill asked and felt the pain each time his jaw moved. He could feel the bruising coming out on his face. He supposed he could do with a little medical attention himself after the brawl with Bear.

'I'll take care of him,' Martha, the hotel owner, said and crossed the room to stand beside the doctor. She was a young woman, not yet out of her thirties. She had been widowed when her husband died the previous summer after falling from his horse and splitting his head open like a ripe melon. Ever since then she had run the only hotel in town single handedly, and done a damn efficient job of it. Far better than any man could, she liked to boast.

Doc Curtis took her hands in his own and smiled. 'Don't bother him too much,' he said. 'Just keep an eye on him and if he wakes, send for me at once.'

She nodded, 'I will, Doc.'

Stanton's two men still looked unsure of the situation and neither man wanted to be the first to leave the room. They stood there along with Bill, Sam, Dutch and Henry. Bear, as far as anyone knew, was still lying outside in the dirt.

'Then if everyone else can leave, the patient needs his rest,' Doc Curtis said and smiled at Martha before scooping his instruments from the bed and placing them into his Gladstone bag.

No one made any sign of moving.

Martha frowned and then clapped her hands together. 'Now, come on,' she said. 'You heard the doc.' She ushered the men out of the room. At first it seemed Stanton's men were about to object but once Bill, Dutch, the sheriff and Henry had gone they followed behind.

Once outside the men split into two camps.

Bill, Dutch, Sam and the kid on one side.

Stanton's men on the other.

Up the street, Bear had now gotten to his feet and as soon as he saw them he walked, stumbled really, towards them. Bill noticed the stocky man looked a wonderful sight after their fight — both his eyes were blackened, his lower lip had swollen to such an extent that it seemed to take up half his face, and there was fresh blood trickling from his nose. Blood had also congealed at the side of his head, and in his hair. Dirt and grit clung to the dried blood. He looked as if a horse had kicked him . . . several horses.

'How you feeling, *boyo?*' Bill asked as the squat man approached them.

Bear's reply was a guttural growl as he ignored Bill and looked at his two comrades for enlightenment. Bill was sure that were it not for all the bruising and dirt, a puzzled expression would have been visible upon his face. One moment he had been fighting and the next everyone's standing around jawing.

'What're we gonna do now?' the sheriff asked. The old man wasn't at all

113

sure of the situation. He had understood the fight and the need to stand firm against Stanton, but now that the head of the Stanton clan was laid up in the hotel, likely as close to death as he'd ever been, he had lost the thread of what was going on. The situation seemed a twist more complicated than it had been only moments ago.

'You're the sheriff.' Bill watched Bear for fear that he would want to resume the fight, but the squat man had no fight left in him.

'And just what would you do if you were sheriff?' the old man asked.

'Guess I might tell these men to leave town,' Bill said. 'They might want to convey the news about old man Stanton to the rest of the clan.'

The sheriff considered that and all its ramifications and he realized that they would have been better off had Stanton ridden out of there in the peach of health. He was the only one of the clan who had any kind of control over that hothead, Caleb. There were two other members of the immediate family but neither Dismas nor Eder Stanton were anything to worry about; they were fat little men with, if one believed the rumours, dubious tastes in young cowhands. No, it was Caleb who was the loose cannon.

'Guess I might do that,' the sheriff said and slid his ancient Dragoon from its holster.

Stanton's men immediately cleared leather but they held their hands when they saw the two other guns held on them. Both Bill and the kid had drawn with a blur of speed, and held their own Colts deadly level. Dutch, at first, seemed unsure of what to do but then he too drew his gun. It wasn't exactly a fast draw but then the end result was very much the same and Stanton's men now found themselves with four guns trained upon them.

The sheriff, realizing that he was now in a position of power, felt mighty proud of himself and his lone tooth gleamed in a mouth stretched wide.

'Now you best go riding on out of town,' he said.

For several tense moments Stanton's men held their ground, but then, as if realizing they had no chance, they turned away. They had to support Bear between them as they made their way to their horses.

15

'You can't go riding in without any men, without any guns,' Caleb said and looked at his uncles. Jake Tanner, who had brought the news from town, stood next to him. He obviously felt awkward and kept his gaze directed at the floor. The altered power dynamic around here seemed to confuse him and he wasn't at all sure if his loyalties should be with Caleb or the elder two Stantons.

'You heard what Jake said,' Caleb continued. 'They've taken over the town, beaten Bear to a pulp and they've got my grandfather.'

'Your grandfather,' Dismas said. 'He's also our father.'

'And no one's got him,' Eder said. 'He's had a heart attack and is being cared for by the town doctor.'

'They're laughing at us,' Caleb positively snarled. 'We jail Henry Carthy, sentence him to be hung, and now he's prancing about town as bold as you like. And that Welshman beats Bear to within an inch of his life. That's probably what brought on Grandfather's heart attack. We should ride into town, take a posse of men in with us, kill them bastards and bring my grandfather home.'

Both Dismas and Eder shook their heads.

'Father had a heart attack,' Dismas said. 'Least it seems that way from what Jake's told us. He's in a hotel bed with the town doctor taking care of him. He's in no danger and going in there shooting is likely to put him in danger.'

Dismas had spoken to him as if he were a child and that enraged Caleb.

'You're a coward,' he said. 'You're both cowards. Fat little cowards.'

'We shall ride into town,' Eder said, firmly, looking to his brother for support. 'We'll see how Father is and decide what to do then. Caleb, you remain here.'

'I'm coming,' Caleb said. 'I'm the

only Stanton with the sand to stand up to these varmints.'

'You stay,' Dismas said. 'You don't think before you act, which is the reason Father went into town without you in the first place. Eder and I will go in alone.'

'Cowards,' Caleb spat the words out. 'You're nothing but cowards.' And with that he swung on his feet, brushed past the three men and went out into the pale afternoon sunshine.

Caleb spotted Clemens standing over by the corral fence. The one-time lawman was chewing on a large cigar, which Caleb guessed he had taken from his grandfather's supply. It certainly had an aroma like the pungent variety the old man often smoked.

'What you gonna do about all this?' Caleb asked as he approached Clemens.

Clemens spat into the dirt and shook his head.

'I ain't sheriff no more,' he said.

Caleb took his makings from his shirt pocket and made himself a quirly.

'What do you think will happen if

Grandfather dies?' he asked and drew hard on the smoke.

Clemens shrugged his shoulders. 'I don't rightly know,' he said. 'These days I don't seem to know much at all.'

'You let that Welshman get the better of you,' Caleb said. 'That's what started this all off.'

Clemens wanted to point out to Caleb that it was he who had set this thing in motion. If he hadn't done whatever it was he had done in the first place, and riled up the Carthy kid then none of this would have happened. Instead he remained silent, nodded and puffed some more on the cigar. He stood there, both feeling and looking like a broken man.

'Yeah,' Caleb said and threw his smoke away, watching as it hit the ground in a shower of sparks. 'And you're gonna help me undo it.'

'Am I?'

Caleb reached out and grabbed the older man by the shirt collar, unbalancing him despite his considerable bulk.

The older, and much bigger man, did nothing and simply stared at Caleb as the much smaller man manhandled him. There was a sad realization in the ex-lawman's eyes and maybe a little resignation too. The realization that he was finished with the Stantons, and that no matter how this thing went, regardless of whether Abaddon Stanton lived or died, it was all over for him. He'd had a position of standing in town and people looked up to him with some sort of respect. The fact it was built on a fear of the Stantons meant little to the man. It was respect nonetheless, but that could never be returned to him. Even if the Welshman was run out of town, or better still killed, and his badge and office returned to him, he would never demand that same respect again.

'Before this day ends,' Caleb said, 'you'll be wearing your badge again.'

'I'd like that,' Clemens said, meekly. There was no real hope in his voice and he knew that there was more to the position of sheriff than pinning a badge to a man's shirt. Caleb needed to face facts — something had been done here that couldn't be undone.

'My uncles are riding into town,' Caleb said. 'They're gonna check on Grandfather. They think they're gonna ride into town and everything will be fine and dandy. They think the town's people and that damn Welshman will take care of the old man, that he won't be harmed.'

'That may be so,' Clemens said.

'My grandfather sentenced Henry Carthy to hang; he fully intended to have the Welshman killed. There ain't any chance they'll leave him unmolested. The town's named Stanton for a reason and I'm going to take it back.'

Clemens said nothing, simply nodded.

'We're gonna take it back,' Caleb insisted. 'As soon as Dismas and Eder return from town, and we find out what the true situation is we'll pull together our best men. We can call it a posse. After all, you're still legally the sheriff and you're gonna help us get back what's ours.'

'There'll be a fight,' Clemens said. 'That Welshman ain't the type to give up and the Carthy kid's as hotheaded as they come. We ride in carrying iron and we'll have to use it.'

'I'm counting on it,' Caleb said and then a bloodless smile, which chilled the other man to the bone, crossed his lips.

'If my grandfather dies, I'll end up running this little empire,' he said. 'Neither Dismas nor Eder have the strength to hold it all together. You know that.'

That was one thing Clemens had to agree with. Neither of Abaddon's sons were up to much as men. It had been his daughter, Caleb's late mother, who had inherited the strength and the ruthless streak that went with the Stanton name. She had passed these traits on to her son, Caleb, but the problem was that where she, like her father, had self control, her son had no such sense. It was as if a red mist descended on Caleb and he went off into a frenzy from which very few people could control him. As far as Clemens knew the only man that could control Caleb was laid up in town after suffering a heart attack.

'And I'll remember my friends,' Caleb said before turning on his feet and heading back to the ranch house. But before he was out of earshot he looked back over his shoulder and added a chilling counterpoint, 'And my enemies.'

16

'Darn strange thing for a fella to do,' Sam said and peered down the barrel of his pistol. Satisfied it was clean he wiped it over with an oily rag and placed it on the desk in front of him. He leaned back in his chair, now feeling at home in the jailhouse-cum-sheriff's office.

'Not where I come from,' Bill said and continued with his knitting. He too was leaning back in his chair and had his feet up on the desk. The two men sat there, side by side, Bill knitting and the sheriff watching as the Welshman skilfully handled the bone knitting needles.

'Make a fine weapon, those,' the old man said, pointed to the needles. They were each about a foot long and tapered down to a fine point.

Bill smiled, said, 'These actually

saved my life at the Little Bighorn.'

'Welsh,' the sheriff said. The old man had taken to calling Bill, Welsh ever since pinning on the tin star. 'You've got sand; I'll give you that. But you do tell a lot of fish tales.'

Once more Bill smiled. 'I was down, wounded,' he said. 'Shot in the shoulder and I think I must have lost consciousness, because one moment the battle was raging and the next I was looking at the desolation that was the battlefield. The Indians called it the Battle of Greasy Grass and as I looked around I realized the name was apt, for the ground was slick with the blood of the fallen. The Indians were scavenging amongst the fallen soldiers, the spoils of war, you know. I knew that if I was discovered still alive I would be swiftly killed, but there was little I could do. I was too weak to try and escape and my wound was still bleeding.' Bill unbuttoned his shirt and exposed his left shoulder, showing a vicious looking scar.

'So what did you do?' the old man asked. He had removed his feet from the desk and now sat bolt upright, captivated by the tale the Welshman was spinning. Of course there were no white survivors of the Bighorn, he knew that, but the Welshman weaved a good story and at times it even seemed convincing.

'There was a dead horse lying next to me, biggest damn horse I'd ever seen. Half its head had been blown away, and as I looked at its swollen stomach I knew I had but one chance. I had no weapons. I had lost them all in the fight; my pistol would have proved useless in any case but I could have done with my sabre. And then I remembered my knitting, which I had placed inside my tunic when the battle had begun.

'Well, I slid one of the needles out; it was one of these I'm using now. And I used it to stab into the horse's stomach. I worked the hole until I could get my fingers in and then I tore the creature's stomach open and removed his guts.

The smell was almost overpowering and I had to swallow the bile back in my throat as I quickly pulled the creature's innards out. I slid myself inside the horse and pulled all the mess back in over me. And then I must have passed out again for when I awoke, and emerged from the horse's belly, the battlefield was deserted and I had only the dead for company. Yep, if it weren't for my knitting needles I wouldn't be here to tell that story now.'

'You hid in an 'orse's belly?'

'I did,' Bill said and shivered at the memory. 'And I don't want to be doing that again any time soon. *Yn diflasu chybola.*'

The old man was about to say something, but whatever it was it was lost forever as Henry came barging in through the heavy front door. The kid stood there in the doorway, while he caught his breath.

'Eder and Dismas Stanton have turned up,' the kid said.

'Abaddon's sons,' the old man said,

noticing Bill's puzzled look.

'And where are they now?' Bill asked.

'They've gone straight to the hotel,' the kid said. 'They came in alone. All on their lonesome and went straight to their father.'

'They had no men with them?' the old man asked.

'They were alone,' the kid repeated. 'They went to the hotel and Martha and the doc let them in.'

'Well I'll be darned,' Sam said, rubbing his chin. 'No men with them. Perhaps we are going to avoid a gunfight after all.'

Bill slid his knitting into his shirt and got to his feet. 'Come on,' he said. 'This is one family reunion I feel we should attend.'

The three men left the jailhouse and crossed the dusty main street. Dutch Carter was standing outside the saloon and he raised a hand in greeting as the three men went by. As soon as they reached the hotel they went inside and were immediately met by Martha. She was standing behind the reception desk and looking through a weighty-looking ledger.

'Hear the old man's got visitors,' Bill said. It wasn't a question.

Martha nodded. 'His sons,' she said. 'They're with him now.'

'How is he?' Bill asked.

'Doc says he's tough enough to pull through.'

'Should have finished him off when we had the chance,' Henry said.

'We ain't murderers,' Bill snapped and once more gave the kid a stern look. He turned back to Martha. 'I'd like to speak to the Stanton boys.'

'You're welcome to wait,' Martha said and indicated for the men to be seated on the bench that ran the length of the reception area. Bill and the sheriff did so but Henry turned and left the hotel in disgust. The sheriff said something about going after the kid and also shuffled out, leaving Bill alone while Martha thumbed through the thick ledger.

Feeling awkward, Bill reached into his pocket and pulled out the makings and quickly made a quirly. He struck a thick match against the underside of the bench and sucked the smoke to life.

'It is kind of you,' Bill said after an awkward silence, smoke drifting between his teeth as he spoke. 'To let the old man stay here.'

'I couldn't leave him dying in the street,' Martha replied without looking up from the ledger. 'And besides, I'm sure I will be paid for the room when Mr Stanton recovers.'

'If he recovers.'

'I'll be paid,' Martha said. 'One way or another I will be paid.'

Once more silence fell between them. The ticking of the clock on the wall became impossibly loud and Bill shifted in his seat. It was Martha who finally broke the silence.

'Why are you doing this?' she asked.

'I don't understand,' Bill replied and stood and went to the door. He opened it, threw the remains of his smoke out into the street and then went back to the bench. He sat back down and noticed Martha was staring at him. She was certainly a beautiful woman and the late afternoon sunshine, filtered through the net curtains as it was, gave her skin a golden glow.

'All this,' Martha said. 'Going against the Stantons. Why?'

'*Paham mo?*' Bill said, and then when Martha gave him a quizzical look, added, 'It means 'why not'?'

'The Stantons have run this town for as long as anyone can remember,' Martha said. 'It was originally called Sweetwater but then it had been nothing more than a few miners' shacks, and it was only when the Stanton family arrived that it started to grow, to prosper. The name was changed to Stanton shortly afterwards and these days the Stantons own half the town, and that which they don't own they don't want.'

'It's not their town, though,' Bill said. 'They don't own the people here. People are not a commodity.'

'They may as well be. They own the homes, the businesses. They charge each and every resident here the town tax, but it's nothing more than extortion. It's not for nothing the town's called Stanton.'

'They own this place?'

'No,' Martha said. 'They don't own this place. I do. They've made offers from time to time, but I always refuse, just as my husband did before his accident. It used to be that windows would get broken or drunken cowboys would come in and smash the place up, but I stood my ground and now I think they've given up on the notion of ever buying me out. My husband bought this place for our future. I'll be dammed if I'm going to let anyone buy me out now that's he's gone.'

'I'm sorry,' Bill said. 'About your husband.'

'He fell from his horse.' For the briefest of moments her eyes clouded over but she took in a deep breath and bit her lower lip. 'He was an expert rider but even the best riders can have accidents. The sheriff said a snake may have startled his horse and caused him to get thrown.'

'You don't believe that?'

'About my husband's accident?'

Bill nodded, 'You don't believe it was an accident?'

Bill thought he detected something in Martha's eyes. There was something that troubled her about her husband's demise, some suspicion that she just couldn't shake off, but before she could answer, the door of the room to her left opened and the doc emerged with two podgy red-haired men. Dismas and Eder Stanton, Bill guessed. He had seen them at that mockery of a trial.

'William Williams,' Bill said, getting to his feet and holding out his hand in greeting.

'The Welshman,' Dismas said, stating the plainly obvious.

'That'll be me,' Bill replied, and smiled wryly as if apologizing for the fact. 'Pleased to make your acquaintance but I do wish it had been under kinder circumstances.'

'My father's asking to see you,' Dismas said and gestured with an arm to the room where Old Man Stanton lay.

'He wants to see me?' Bill hadn't meant to give the question voice. 'You think I'd be the last person he wanted to see.'

'Nevertheless,' Dismas said. 'He wishes to speak with you.'

Bill and Martha exchanged looks and then Bill nodded.

'I'll take you in,' the doc said and grabbed Bill's arm and led him through to the room where the old man lay recovering. Or dying — no one seemed really sure which.

17

The man in the bed looked totally different to the man who had presided over the farce of a trial. Then he had seemed strong and although aged, there had been vitality in his eyes, and yet now he looked frail, weak, as if each breath could be his last. His skin was pallid and his cheekbones sunken so that his face resembled that of a corpse. It was as if he was already dead but hadn't yet realized the fact.

Bill cleared his throat.

'Mr Stanton,' he said.

The old man opened his eyes but was unable to move his head and they remained focused on the ceiling.

'Williams?' he asked, his voice sounding gossamer thin.

'Aye,' Bill said.

'Come closer.'

Bill looked at the doc, who nodded.

Bill moved closer, standing over the bed. Abaddon's skin looked yellow, like old parchment, and his eyes rheumy.

'You can leave us alone, Doc,' the old man said.

At first the doctor looked unsure but then he nodded to Bill, held up a hand to signify five minutes and then left the room.

'How are you then?' Bill asked.

A hint of a smile crossed the old man's lips.

'You want money?' he asked.

'The twelve hundred dollars you stole from me would be welcome.'

'I stole nothing.'

'Semantics,' Bill said. 'Then the twelve hundred you levied from me in court fines wouldn't go amiss.'

'A piffle,' the old man said and coughed weakly.

'To you, maybe,' Bill said. 'But it represents a considerable sum to me. Have you any idea of how long it took me to raise a stake like that?'

'I can give you twice that,' the old

man said. 'Thrice even.'

'And what would I have to do for such a sum?'

For a moment there was silence and the old man closed his eyes. For a second Bill thought he had fallen back asleep, or even died, but then he spoke again.

'I am an old man and, as you can see, I am not in the best of health. Only a few years ago I would have come down hard on you for what you have done.' The old man coughed, more violently this time. Bill was about to fetch the doc when Abaddon lifted an arm. 'Wait.'

'Look, Mr Stanton,' Bill said but something in the old man's manner stopped him.

'Hear me out,' Abaddon managed and weakly wiped the spittle from his lips.

'I don't think you should be exerting yourself,' Bill said.

'Help me,' Abaddon said. 'Prop up my pillows. It will be easier if I can look you in the eyes.'

'*Duw duw*,' Bill said. 'I don't think that's very wise.'

'Just do it,' Abaddon said and even in his weakened state his frail voice carried authority.

'*Ar eich pen yn ei*,' Bill warned but did what the old man said. He gently lifted Abaddon's head, disgusted by the clammy feel of his skin, and pulled the feather pillows up. Then he lowered the old man back down again. 'I really don't think this is wise.'

'You talk too much,' the old man said. 'Please do a dying man the courtesy of shutting up. Let me speak.'

'Well, go on then,' Bill said and sat down on the edge of the bed. The room was growing dim now as the afternoon gave way to evening. Soon it would be night and Bill considered it a distinct possibility that it could prove to be Abaddon's last.

'I built this town,' Abaddon said. 'When I came here it was nothing more than a mining camp. The saloon, the bank and the jailhouse were all built with my money. I had the dam that feeds this land constructed. Before that dam redirected the waters this town was nothing more than a dust bowl. The bones of both my wife and daughter lie beneath the soil and soon mine will be beside them. If it were not for me this town would have died long ago.'

'So I've heard,' Bill said, taking the old man's pause as an opportunity to contribute to the conversation. It wasn't that he had that much to say, but he had always felt awkward if he remained silent for too long. Bill could never be called the strong silent type; he knew that and considered himself to be more of the tenacious, talkative variety.

'You said you would hear me out.'

'Sorry.'

A silence fell between them, the old man's eyes closed and for a moment Bill thought once again that he had fallen asleep, but then the eyes snapped open.

'I'm tired,' he said.

'I'll go,' Bill got to his feet.

'No, stay,' Abaddon started to cough again, his chest sounding as if each breath could be his last. 'I just need a moment.'

The door opened and Dismas and Eder Stanton stood in the doorway, they both looked suspiciously at Bill for a moment and then turned to their father on the bed.

'Shall we wait?' Dismas asked.

'No,' the old man said. 'Go and keep Caleb under control.'

The two men didn't question their father and immediately closed the door just as the old man went into another coughing fit.

'My sons,' the old man said presently, wiping spittle from the back of his lips with a hand. 'They are weak. Quite useless.'

Bill nodded, said nothing.

'Where was I?' the old man closed his eyes again, searching his mind for his train of thought.

'You were telling me how you practically built this town,' Bill helpfully informed him.

'Indeed,' the old man said. 'I did and more than that. I've made it a decent place for people to live, a safe place. In order to do that I've often had to make difficult decisions, and at times I've had to use force to maintain law and order.'

'How did having the kid hung and me shot help with your law and order?' Bill asked. The old man may have been gravely ill, but Bill was getting tired of this self-righteous tripe. From what he could tell Abaddon Stanton was nothing more than a dictator who crushed anyone and everyone who stood in his way.

'Sometimes I have made mistakes,' the old man said. 'That is inevitable in law. The court found Henry Carthy guilty of attempted murder and the death penalty is just is such cases.'

'I was charged with being a transient,' Bill said. 'Was murdering me just?'

'I am willing to admit a mistake has

been made,' Abaddon said, ignoring the finer points of the Welshman's question. 'The law is not infallible.'

'Your law is no law,' Bill said. 'I've known men like you before. You've murdered people behind the colour of the law.'

'I am the judge in this town,' Abaddon said, his voice rising, which clearly wasn't good for him in his current position, and yet again he went into a spasm of coughing. Afterwards he lay there, breathing deeply while he regained his breath.

'There's little use in skirting the issue,' Abaddon said, presently. 'I'll get straight to the point.'

'I do wish you would,' Bill said. He wasn't comfortable being here with the old man like this. True, Stanton was frail and probably didn't have that much time left to him, but only days ago he had sentenced both Henry and Bill to death — Henry by the rope and Bill by an assassin's bullet in the back. The old man didn't deserve any sympathy and he certainly wasn't going to get it from the Welshman.

The old man smiled, weakly. 'If you remain here,' he said, 'there will be bloodshed, regardless of what happens to me. My sons may be weak but my grandson, Caleb, is not so. He is young, foolish, and impulsive. He thinks every problem can be solved with a gun and he has a small army of men at his disposal. The longer I am here the more difficult it will be to keep him under control.'

'Let him come,' Bill said. 'I have never run from a fight and I see no reason to start now. As my *da* used to say, *ynmgryma achos na ddyn*. Bow down for no man.'

'Very poetic,' Abaddon said. 'But we have men, many men and you are few. Too few.'

'I have all I need,' Bill retorted.

'Three thousand dollars American,' Abaddon said, and allowed the words to hang on the air before continuing. 'I will give you that sum. To be used as you see fit.'

Three thousand American, was a

fortune. A truly life-changing amount of money and momentarily the gambler within Bill considered what he could do with such a stake. But it was only for a fleeting moment and Bill knew he would never accept such a sum from a man like this. He had his pride and to take the money would be to turn his back on everything he had ever believed in. It would be a blow to the principles he tried to live by.

'All I want is my twelve hundred back,' Bill said.

'Forget the twelve hundred. I will give you three thousand. All you have to do is leave town,' Abaddon said. 'Take the kid and that fool old man playing sheriff with you. You can give the money to them for all I care. Just go.'

'No deal,' Bill said and then stood up.

'You have an inflated opinion of yourself,' the old man said. 'You make the deal, you live and get rich. You don't and you die a poor man.'

'No deal,' Bill repeated.

He turned to Abaddon, knelt over the bed and looked the old man directly in the eye. He no longer had anything to gain from holding back, since by now Thomson would have reached Fort Hood and would most likely be on the way back with soldiers, maybe even the US marshall. Stanton's empire was crumbling just as the old man himself now withered.

'It's over for you,' Bill said. 'I've sent for the US marshall. He will be on his way here by now and I fully expect that by noon tomorrow there will be real law in Stanton.'

The old man looked at him, searching the Welshman's eyes for signs of a bluff but somehow he knew that this was no poker face. The Welshman was telling the truth and knowing the details didn't matter.

'Bastard,' Abaddon said and then closed his eyes.

There was nothing more to say.

18

It was a clear night.

Bill felt uneasy, as if someone was hiding in the shadows, as he crossed the street and made his way to the saloon. He knew he was being jumpy but nevertheless he was relieved to push open the batwings and step inside.

The saloon was busy and the atmosphere seemed easy. Laughter, singing — people were having a good time and Bill suspected much of that was to do with the fact that the Stantons no longer appeared invincible. The patriarch of the family was close to death's door and Bill and his companion had stood up to him and his men, seemingly coming away the victors. It felt as if an oppressive cloud had been lifted from the town. There was even talk, Bill had heard from Dutch Carter, of changing the name of the town. Someone had apparently suggested Williamstown in Bill's honour.

Bill spotted the kid stood against the counter, nursing a beer, and he pushed his way over to him.

'Howdy, Welsh,' the kid said by way of greeting. Like Sam the kid had taken to calling Bill, 'Welsh'. When Bill merely smiled the kid added: 'So?'

'So?'

'So what's happening? Is Old Man Stanton dead yet?'

'I'll have a beer please,' Bill said, ignoring the question. While the kid waved to get the barkeep's attention, he looked around the saloon and saw Sam standing talking to a couple of cowboys in the far corner. Sam was waving his hands about as he spoke to illustrate whatever point he was trying to make. He was clearly relishing being a lawman. He had polished the tin star he wore on his shirt to such an extent that it sparkled every time the light hit it.

'Beer,' the kid slapped the glass on the counter before Bill. 'Well?' he prompted.

'*Duw*, that hit the spot.' Bill placed his glass back down on the counter. 'Well, I think our troubles with the Stantons may all be over.'

'The old man's dead then?'

'No, he ain't dead. Though I don't expect he has much longer left. He's gravely ill and he knows it's all over for him. The US Marshall will arrive tomorrow, the day after at the latest. The Stantons' reign is over.'

'Just like that?'

'Just like that,' Bill nodded and took another sip of his beer. 'Maybe if the old man hadn't have suffered the heart attack he would have rallied some men together, and gone against us. But as it stands he has bigger issues to face — likely he'll die.'

'What about his family?'

'His sons won't make any trouble,' Bill said. 'And his grandson, your *buttie*, Caleb, is being kept on a tight leash. It's over and as soon as the real law arrives I guess I'll move on.'

'I've still got a score to settle with

Caleb,' the kid said.

'Ahh yes,' Bill smiled. 'That's what started all this. Tell me, what exactly did Caleb do?'

'I told you already.'

'No. You said he disrespected your mother. Tell me, how did he do that?'

The kid drained his beer and was just about to speak when gunfire sounded from the far corner of the saloon. Bill almost jumped from his skin and the beer that had been on the way to his mouth ended up over his shirtfront. He dropped the glass and in one fluid movement cleared leather, spun on his heels and had his weapon ready to fire. He noticed the kid had drawn quicker, and was already looking into the pandemonium that had erupted.

'Sheriff,' Bill shouted.

Confusion followed. Nobody was dispersing as was to be expected but instead everyone in the saloon seemed to be surging forward to one corner of the saloon, fighting to get a view of what was happening. Bill pushed into the crowd, followed by the kid, but they made no progress until Bill set off a shot into the ceiling, plaster falling down like snow in the air, and the crowd parted.

Bill saw Sam on the floor, cursing, rolling about and clutching a foot, which was spurting blood through the scorched leather of his boot.

'Sheriff?' Bill looked at the old man in confusion. He and the kid shared puzzled glances and then moved forward as one.

'Shot my darn foot,' the sheriff said. 'Darn it hurts.'

Bill returned his Colt to leather.

So did the kid.

'Someone bring the doc,' Bill shouted and bent to help the old man.

'He was showing off,' a bearded man with only one eye explained. He ran the back of a hand over his mouth and spat tobacco juice on to the floor. 'Demonstrating what he called, *'his new lawman way of drawing his gun'*. Loco old coot.'

'Deke Hawkins,' Sam said through gritted teeth. 'I just might shoot you next.'

'That'll be the day,' the bearded man said and shook his head before wandering off to the counter to get another drink. The stench of cordite hung heavy in the air and seemed to be stimulating the thirst of many of those here. There was a sudden rush for the counter.

'You sure killed your foot,' the kid said, then grinned, and went off to get a drink of his own.

'My darn gun's faulty,' Sam said as a fresh wave of pain set his nerve endings alight. 'Someone get me a whiskey.'

'It's not whiskey you need, you old fool,' the doc said as he pushed his way through the crowd and knelt down beside the old man. He opened his everpresent bag and clucked his tongue against the roof of his mouth. 'Damn fool.'

Bill smiled and left the doc to administer to his patient while he too went in search of another drink.

19

Caleb had never felt such rage. It seemed to start at the very core of his being and radiate out in every direction, setting his blood boiling and his nerves on fire. He clenched his fists in fury, so tightly that his nails dug into the palms of his hands and the veins running along his arms bulged purple. He wanted to shoot someone, anyone, set off a full chamber into someone's gut, screaming his anger as each and every slug tore flesh and ruined organs. He kicked out at a discarded bucket, sending it crashing into the corral fence, and stormed towards the bunk-house.

Dawn was still some hours off as he entered the bunkhouse and he had to light the oil lamp that hung inside the doorway before he could see anything other than shadows.

'Get up,' he yelled. 'Each and every one of you.' And with that he turned on his feet and headed back to the house, leaving a bunch of mighty confused ranch-hands scrambling about in the semi-darkness.

Dismas and Eder were asleep in their rooms upstairs and Caleb didn't want to wake them. He didn't need them for what he had in mind. Indeed, he knew they would try and stop him, just as they had tried to talk him out of his plan of action when they had returned from town the previous night.

It was their opinion that nothing should be done other than wait for their father to recover. Then and only then would the problems in town be addressed. In the meantime the Welsh-man and Henry Carthy, both men who had been tried and convicted by the Stanton court, would be allowed to wander about as they pleased. That stuck in Caleb's craw and the best option as far as he was concerned was to let his uncles sleep, and then by the time they woke, neither of them being early risers, he planned on being back from town with his grandfather safely recovering in his own bed and Clemens reinstated as town sheriff. The Welshman and that damn Henry Carthy would be dead and let anyone say anything about that. Those two had to be killed if the Stanton authority was to ever mean anything again. What his two fat uncles failed to realize was that every second that the Welshman and the kid wandered around, seemingly without a care in the world, the Stantons' position in the town was weakened.

Clemens had been given the guest room on the ground floor and Caleb went directly there and threw the door open. He heard the fat man snoring and he shook his head. No wonder the Welshman had gained the upper hand with Clemens if he didn't even stir when someone came charging into his bedroom.

'Wake up,' Caleb said.

'What is it?' Clemens sat up, staring through bleary eyes at the shadowy figure of Caleb standing in the doorway. He reached over to the bedside table and took a match to the lamp. 'What's the matter?'

'Get your clothes on,' Caleb said. 'Wear your guns. We're riding into town.'

'Why?' Clemens asked yet again. He rubbed sleep from his eyes and searched for his watch, which was hanging from its chain and still attached to his shirt that he'd tossed over the chair beside the bed: 3.30 a.m. What could be so all-fire important to wake him at his ungodly hour? 'What's happened?'

'Get up, fat man,' Caleb said. 'I won't tell you again. Be outside in ten minutes and ready to ride.'

Clemens looked at Caleb but said nothing. There had been a time when Caleb would never have had the gall to talk to him like that, but a lot of things had changed lately and Clemens knew that if Old Man Stanton died and his grandson did take over, then things would be mighty different around here.

Caleb looked at Clemens and shook his head in disgust. He left the room, closed the door behind him and went back to the bunkhouse where twenty men were now awake and waiting for him.

Caleb hadn't slept more than an hour. He had kept tossing and turning through the night, his mind refusing to let go of the fury he felt towards the Welshman and the kid. He felt equal fury for his uncles who had returned from town with the news that their father was weak. They claimed that his orders were for nothing to be done until he was well enough to decide the correct course of action.

They had told Caleb that there had been a meeting between his grandfather and the Welshman, which only served to infuriate him even further. His grandfather was a big man, an important man and this Welshman was nothing, just another saddle-tramp.

There was only one way to handle this situation. Caleb knew that and he was sure that his grandfather knew it also. The fact that he had seemingly ordered Dismas and Eder otherwise suggested that the old man was not in full control. Maybe his illness was clouding his judgement, or maybe he was trying to protect his family by ensuring nothing was done until he was ready and able to do it himself.

'Get your weapons,' Caleb said as he went back into the bunkhouse. 'Pistols and rifles. We're heading into town.'

He was answered by puzzled expressions across the faces of every man present. It was the ranch foreman who stepped forward to question Caleb.

'What's happened?' Jake asked.

'We're going to get my grandfather,' Caleb said. 'And kill that damn Welshman.'

'But — ' Jake started but his words were cut off when Bear pushed past him and went and stood besides Caleb.

'The Welshman's mine,' Bear said.

'You can have him,' Caleb said and a cold grin crossed his face. 'After I've finished with him.'

20

'This don't feel right,' Clemens said, looking at Jake who rode besides him. Behind them were another twenty heavily armed men and ahead of them rode Caleb and Bear. It felt to Clemens that he was riding as part of an army, which he supposed to all intents and purposes, he was.

Caleb clearly aimed to take them into battle.

'I know what you mean,' Jake said, shifting in his saddle. 'But without Mr Stanton around, I guess that means Cal's in charge.'

'You think this is what Abaddon would do?'

Jake shrugged. 'Beats me,' he said. 'Then I'm just a hired hand and I do what I'm told.'

'It's insane,' Clemens grumbled. 'I know Mr Stanton better than any man and he wouldn't do this.'

'It's been done before,' Jake pointed out.

Clemens knew what Jake was referring to. Maybe ten years ago, just after the war, a group of home-steaders displaced by the battles in the South had set up a camp on the meadows to the east of the town. The Stantons had previously ignored the land that stretched away towards the Ruthless Mountains like an ocean of tall grasses, but as soon as Abaddon discovered the settlers he had decided that it was his land and that the newcomers were trespassing. At first the settlers had been told they had to pay rent and then when they refused they had been warned off, told to move on, and then threatened when they failed to heed the warnings. Still the settlers stood firm and so more direct action had been taken. The camp had been raided one night; the single building that had been constructed was taken to the torch and razed to the ground. No one had been hurt but cattle had been run off and stock destroyed.

Clemens had been involved in that raid, which was something that still troubled him from time to time. Using the badge of office, he'd served papers on the settlers, papers that had ordered them to vacate the land, which they were illegally occupying. He'd known the legality of the papers, which had been drawn up by Abaddon himself, was questionable but he'd served them anyway. And when the men had ridden roughshod through the camp, destroying property and running off or killing livestock, he had taken part, had been among the riders.

The settlers, though, had been tenacious and had challenged Abaddon's claim to the land, threatening to bring in the US marshall's office to make a ruling on the matter. It didn't get that far because one night a group of unknown riders rode into the camp and shot dead three men and a woman. After that the settlers, or what was left of them, moved on. No one ever did find out who the gunmen were. Well not for certain, in any case, but deep down Clemens knew that whoever they were they had been acting on Abaddon Stanton's orders.

'Things are changing,' Clemens said, presently. 'The West is becoming civilized and it ain't so easy to use a gun to solve problems any more. There's other law besides Stanton law.'

'Maybe it won't come to any blood,' Jake said, though without any real conviction in his words. 'Maybe Cal will ride in and pick up his grandfather and then ride out again. No one need get killed.'

'You don't believe that any more than I do,' Clemens said.

'Nope,' Jake had to agree. 'Don't suppose I do.'

Clemens frowned and fell silent. He knew he had lost control of events and that he was being dragged along to a conclusion that was terrifying. There was something about the Welshman that troubled Clemens and he knew that the man wouldn't be easily defeated. He was too smart for that and if it came to a fight Clemens suspected that the Welshman was more than a match for any man among them. What Caleb and Abaddon before him had failed to realize is that this Welshman was like no man they had ever come across.

The sky was breaking up as the false dawn was fast becoming a reality, and there was enough visibility to see the town of Stanton in the distance. Clemens shivered as they neared the town and an oppressive cloud seemed to settle over him.

21

Ordinarily Bill wasn't an early riser and would often sleep in until well into the morning. He couldn't remember the last time he had seen the dawn arrive and yet that morning, for some reason, he had awoken before the sun had even put in an appearance. Of course, the bunk in the jailhouse, which served as his bed, wasn't the most comfortable, but that didn't bother him none and was nothing to do with his being up and about so early. The sheriff had slept in the next bunk, with his bandaged foot supported by a cushion — Bill had never known a man make so much noise in his sleep. For the entire night the old man had been either snoring or farting, often both together. He'd also slapped his mouth together at regular intervals and quite often it had been a combination of all three.

Though Bill knew he couldn't blame the old man for his sleepless night; he had slept through much worse in the past. Indeed Bill's folks had often joked that he would sleep through the end of the world.

Bill was fully expecting Thomson to return sometime that morning, more than likely with soldiers or the law in tow, and he guessed that might have had something to do with him being up and about. The Welshman was now eager to ride on from this town. He'd been here quite long enough and just as soon as he felt able to leave, he planned on doing so.

Upon waking he'd gone to the stove and after coaxing the dying embers back to life by blowing gently through cupped hands and feeding it a couple of Wanted posters he'd found in the drawers, (*Gary Dobbs, for passing counterfeit notes and despoiling a preacher's daughter, and Arkansas Smith, dead or alive, for bank robbery and murder*) he had thrown on some sticks then brewed a pot of coffee.

And now with dawn starting to paint the sky in crimson stripes, he sat on the bench outside the jailhouse, a tin mug of coffee beside him, while he concentrated on his knitting. Bill did so like to knit and although other men would often josh him over it, he would smile knowingly. For Bill knew something that they didn't; that there were other benefits besides the obvious to his knitting. The deft way he worked the needles kept his fingers nimble and, he was sure, improved the speed of his draw and there wasn't a man alive who could josh the Welshman about the speed of his draw.

The town was starting to awake now and Bill saw the hotel door open and then Martha came outside carrying a pail of trash, which she emptied into the large steel drum that she had positioned to the side of, and downwind of, her building. He wrapped his knitting around his needles and then slid them inside his shirt.

'It's gonna be a lovely day,' he said as

he walked over to Martha. 'How is Mr Stanton this morning?'

Martha smiled and wiped the back of a hand across her brow.

'He seems stronger,' she said.

'That is good.'

'I've just fixed him breakfast,' Martha said and then added as if an afterthought. 'Would you like a little breakfast yourself?'

'I don't want to put you to any trouble.'

'No trouble,' Martha replied. 'I've got no other guests at the moment and I've fried up plenty of bacon. It's no trouble.'

The thought of a real breakfast was certainly enticing and Bill felt his stomach cartwheel at the suggestion. Left to his own devices all he would have had would have been the coffee and maybe a stale biscuit.

'*Ddiolch* ch,' Bill said. 'Thank you.'

'Then come on,' Martha said. 'Or it'll get cold.'

And it did prove to be a nourishing

breakfast. Served in the kitchen at the rear of the hotel, Bill was faced with freshly cooked bacon, three eggs, a generous helping of beans and a mound of fried potatoes. He couldn't remember the last time he'd eaten such a meal and the coffee he washed the food down with was far sweeter than that he'd drunk earlier.

'You enjoyed that,' Martha observed, watching Bill as he mopped his plate with a thick piece of bread.

'I did,' Bill nodded and mouthed the bread that was now dripping with juice. He chewed it for several moments and then swallowed noisily before finishing off his coffee.

'More coffee?' Martha asked, taking the cup from him. She went to the pot beside the stove and poured herself a cup as well as refilling Bill's. She returned and sat at the table opposite him. 'You've a healthy appetite,' she said and sipped delicately at her own coffee.

Bill gulped down his own and then wiped his mouth with one of the napkins Martha had placed on the table.

'I've not eaten so good since leaving my home,' Bill said. 'I never thought I'd taste cooking as good as my dear old mum's, but I must say this meal you set before me came pretty darn close.'

'I'm pleased you enjoyed it,' Martha said and started collecting the dirty dishes. She carried them over to the sink and placed them on the side. She went back to the table and sat back down, deciding she had enough time to finish her coffee.

'I must pay you,' Bill said.

'You certainly will not,' Martha snapped.

'Maybe I could do some chores,' Bill suggested.

'You can finish your coffee,' Martha replied. 'And say no more about it.'

Bill was amazed at how comfortable he felt just sitting here with this woman. She was little more than a stranger to him and yet there was none of the awkwardness which was usual when alone with someone you didn't really know. It felt good to Bill, almost if he belonged.

He was about to say something but he was silenced by the sound of a forceful rapping on the hotel door. He stood with Martha and followed her through to the front of the building. The rapping on the door continued, growing more powerful.

'I'm coming,' Martha said. 'Leave the door on its hinges.'

Bill felt a sense of dread rising up from the pit of his being and somehow he knew, before the door was even opened, it would be Caleb standing outside.

22

'What's he doing here?' Caleb asked.

'What are *you* doing here?' Bill threw back.

'I'm here to see my grandfather,' Caleb looked suspiciously at Martha and then turned his attention back to Bill. There was a look of hatred in his eyes and they seemed to glow as red as his thick thatch of hair.

Bill looked beyond Caleb at the riders gathered outside. Bill counted twelve men through the doorway. There would be more out there that he couldn't see.

'You've come heavy handed for a visit,' he said.

'Where's my grandfather?' Caleb asked. 'If you've hurt him — '

'Your grandfather's fine,' Martha said. 'And I won't tolerate raised voices in my hotel.'

'I'll be outside,' Bill said and stepped

past Caleb and out through the door. He looked at the men gathered there. There were more than twenty men, all armed, and he noticed Clemens, the one-time sheriff among them. He also recognized Bear who was sat on a horse to his far left. The man's face was a mass of cuts and bruises and when he caught Bill's stare, the Welshman noticed that several of his teeth were now missing.

Caleb had come into town in force and Bill realized that there would be bloodshed before this was all over. This was it, it was inevitable, and there was no other way it could end. Yesterday, when Eder and Dismas Stanton had come into town, they had been alone, but Caleb had come with a small army. A man with such force behind him would be eager for a fight and intent on having one.

'You all come visiting?' Bill asked but received no reply from any of the riders. He saw people crossing the street up ahead and making for cover. The town had woken up to the realization that the long-threatened showdown was about to occur.

Bill was at a loss as to what to do and he simply stood there trying not to look too nervous, which took considerable self-control since the sight of all these armed men terrified him. He wondered how long Thomson would take getting there with help and decided that now would be a good time for him to arrive . . . a very good time.

Bill saw the kid coming across the street towards them. Behind the kid, Sam hobbled along, a crutch jammed beneath one arm, his injured foot heavily bandaged. Despite all this, though, the old coot was ready for a fight and he held his oversized pistol in one of his hands.

'You sure do seem to attract trouble, Welsh,' the kid said as he jumped up on the boardwalk and stood beside Bill. He stared at each of the riders before them in turn and then smiled recklessly. 'Reckon I could take most of these on my own,' he said and allowed his hands to brush his Colts, which provoked movement from several of the riders.

No one went for a gun but they all seemed to ready themselves to do so. A few of the riders continued to fidget uneasily in their saddles but no one said anything. They remained silent when the now-crippled sheriff came over, cursing with each and every step.

'What's going on here?' he asked.

'They're just visiting their boss,' Bill said. 'Only they seem to have brought lead instead of flowers.'

'First one of you buzzards move and I'll blow you clean into the afterlife,' the sheriff said, shaking the Dragoon about so as to illustrate his point. 'Any gunplay in my town and I'll be the one playing it.'

Bill smiled. Since putting on the tin star the old man had certainly developed sand. Though he wished he wouldn't wave his gun about like that as there was no telling what he would shoot next.

'We don't want no trouble,' Clemens said. He addressed this directly towards Bill, who he obviously saw as the leader.

'You ain't sheriff no more,' Sam retorted. 'I am. And if there's any trouble to be giving then I'll be the one giving it. I may only have one leg but I can still whip any of you buzzards.'

'I'm gonna kill you, old man,' Bear snarled and shifted in his saddle as though going for the rifle in the boot. Immediately Bill and the kid cleared leather and pointed their weapons at the squat man, but Bear simply smiled. 'And you, Welshman. I'm gonna kill you slowly.'

'Make one more move and you'll be the first to die,' Bill said. 'And besides you had your chance and only ended up losing your teeth.'

Several men laughed at that but were silenced by Bear's glare. The squat man gripped his reins until his knuckles glowed a bony white.

'You think the three of you have a

chance against so many?' the speaker was Jake Tanner.

'Maybe not,' the kid answered. 'But I reckon we can get a good many of you before we go down. And you'll be the first I go for.'

'Indeed,' Bill agreed. 'The question is, do any of you want to try your hand?'

Bill knew that they didn't stand a chance against so many men and it was likely that if gunfire sounded, he, the kid and the old man would die in a hail of hot lead. There were just too many men, but he was confident nothing would happen just yet. At least, not until Caleb came out and instigated events.

It was then that Dutch Carter joined them on the boardwalk. He was visibly terrified but nevertheless he was ready to stand besides the three men. He smiled weakly at Bill and then opened his jacket at the waist to show he was heeled.

'Our numbers seem to be increasing,'

Bill said. He was trying to feign indifference but he was inwardly quaking, which was good. Fear would give him an edge and although there was no chance of him surviving should a fight break out, he knew that he wouldn't go down easily.

For now, though, it was a standoff.

23

Caleb came away from the window and stood directly over his grandfather's bed.

'I've enough men out there to kill them all,' he argued. 'We've got justification. Clemens is with us and in truth he's still legally the sheriff. If the Welshman and his bunch resist arrest, which they will, we can quite lawfully shoot them down. We can get you home, you can get well and things'll pretty soon return to normal.'

'No,' Abaddon said. 'I've told you. No more. It's over.'

'It's our town,' Caleb said, conscious not to raise his voice and bring the woman in to investigate. The woman, Martha she was called, seemed to have taken it upon herself to act as nursemaid to his grandfather, which was ironic given that the Stantons were responsible for her husband's death. She didn't know that, of course, not for certain, but she must have had her suspicions.

'It's not important,' Abaddon said. 'Not any more.'

'You can't let these men get away with this. We've got standing in this town. The name Stanton means something.'

'Enough, I've said,' the old man felt a stab of pain in his chest and he gritted his teeth. He breathed slowly and deeply, which eased things a little.

'You're weak,' Caleb continued. 'You'll feel differently when you recover.' He went back to the window and parted the curtains to look outside. He could see the Welshman and the three men with him on the boardwalk. He could simply take out his gun and fire from here, blow the Welshman's head off before anyone knew what was happening. And that would be that.

'It's that Welshman,' he said. 'Kill him and the others will fall apart.'

'Go back to the ranch,' Abaddon said and closed his eyes. 'It's all over.'

Caleb turned and looked at his grandfather, and he knew at that moment that things would never be the same again. The old man was past it. He had no strength left and would never again be able to rule the town in quite the same way as he once had. Even if he did recover and his strength returned, he had lost the will to lead. Abaddon Stanton was finished, but Caleb was damned if he'd leave it at that. The Stantons practically owned the town. They took in a lot of money in taxes from the town's people and there was no way Caleb would allow that to be jeopardized. Why should he? It was his inheritance; he had been born to take over the empire his grandfather had forged. And take over he would, but first the Welshman had to be killed regardless of what his grandfather said.

'You ain't thinking straight,' Caleb said. 'You've had a close brush with death and it's drained you. Not that long back you would have skinned the Welshman alive for challenging you. You sentenced Henry Carthy to be hung and he's strutting about out there like a rooster. Won't be long before everyone else in the town starts challenging us. Is that what you want?'

Abaddon looked at his grandson. The boy reminded him so much of his late daughter, the boy's mother. He had the same determined manner but Caleb was foolish with it and Abaddon knew he could never take over and maintain the Stantons' rule. When Abaddon died the Stanton name would lose its power over the people of the town. Dismas and Eder were too weak and whilst Caleb possessed the necessary strength, he didn't have the intelligence.

'Just go,' Abaddon said. 'I want to sleep.'

Caleb walked back over to the bed and looked down at his grandfather.

The old man was already dead, or may as well have been because he had lost his spirit. The time had come for Caleb to take over the running of the family empire and he was ready to assume that responsibility. The problem was, Caleb knew that none of the men would follow him whilst the old man was still alive and telling them otherwise. All of the men were loyal to Abaddon and would never go against his word.

'I'll go,' he said. 'But not until you do.'

Caleb reached for a pillow and pulled it roughly from beneath his grandfather's head. The old man's eyes opened, startled. Then Caleb placed the pillow over his face and pushed down. The old man struggled but Caleb merely pressed the pillow down harder and held it there until the old man's struggles ceased and he lay perfectly still.

'Sorry, Grandfather,' Caleb said and gently lifted the old man's head and placed the pillow back beneath him. 'You died before I killed you in any case.'

Caleb walked from the room and was met by Martha. She was carrying a tray upon which sat a pitcher of water and a couple of glasses. She smiled at him but the gesture vanished when she saw the look on his face. She would later think that there was an icy coldness in his eyes and maybe a little madness.

'He's dead,' Caleb said.

'But,' Martha dropped the tray. The pitcher smashed, spilling water everywhere. 'He seemed to be getting better.'

'He's dead,' Caleb repeated. 'And it was that Welshman that killed him. Just as if he'd put a bullet in his head, he killed him.'

Martha went into the bedroom, needing to see for herself. She looked down at the old man. He looked as if his last moments had been spent in agony and she guessed he had suffered another heart attack. She buried her face in her hands and started to weep.

Caleb looked at her through the doorway, puzzled by the woman's show of emotion. It was Abaddon who had ordered her husband killed; they took a good chunk of her earnings as tax and yet she wept as if the old man's passing was a personal loss to her. He just couldn't figure it out.

'They'll pay for this,' Caleb said.

'It was his heart,' Martha replied without looking up from the old man. 'He's at peace now.'

'There'll be no peace until that Welshman is laying dead beside him.'

'You're angry,' Martha said. 'It's natural. It'll pass.'

Caleb ignored her, went to the main door and stepped outside on to the boardwalk. His gun hung limply by his side and for a moment he kept his head bowed, looking at his own feet. He was aware that all eyes were upon him and he was doubly aware of how close the Welshman and his men were to him. They were bunched together, the four of them.

'What's happening?' Clemens asked. 'Is Abaddon coming back with us?'

Caleb didn't answer, remained silent and kept his gaze directed downwards.

'What's happening?' Clemens repeated. 'Is your grandfather OK?

Caleb did then look up. He looked Clemens directly in the eye and then his gaze shifted along the line of his men and finally came to rest on Bill and the three men who stood with him.

'Grandfather's dead,' Caleb said. 'They killed him.'

Immediately, as the shock of his words took effect, Caleb pulled his Schofield and fired.

It was then that all hell broke loose.

24

Caleb's shot had taken two men down.

Not aimed, and slung off in the general direction of the four men the bullet went through Dutch Carter's cheek, emerged the other end with a splatter of gore, and then took the top of Sam's head off. Carter screamed blood and fell to his knees while the sheriff was thrown sideways, dead instantly.

Instinctively Bill dived for the ground and rolled himself towards the riders, spooking their horses so they wouldn't be able to get off a clean shot at him. At the same time, while he rolled in the dirt he cleared leather and shot into the melee of panicked horses and cursing riders. As soon as he was able to get to his feet he did so, and, sending off several shots over his shoulder he ducked beside the hotel. A slug splintered the wood of the hotel wall as he disappeared from view. He'd felt the thing whistle past his head, missing him by the length of a gnat's whisker.

Bill was confused as to what had happened. He knew Caleb had sent off a wild shot but after that it was all a blur. He had seen the old man go down. There could be no mistake of that since a good portion of his head had splattered the side of Bill's face. But as to the fate of Dutch and the kid, Bill was not so sure. He heard gunfire, so obviously someone was fighting back.

Hugging the wall of the hotel with his back, a Colt in each hand, he was just about to look around the building when one of the riders appeared around the corner. The rider saw Bill and went for his rifle but the Welshman was quicker and the rider took a slug dead centre of his chest and fell from his saddle. His horse bolted in Bill's direction and Bill leapt in front of the creature, held his hands up and managed to stop it.

He pulled himself into the saddle.

Bill sent the terrified animal into a gallop, heading around to the front of the hotel. He fired off at random and saw another of Stanton's men blown out of the saddle. It was chaos and no one seemed at all sure whom they were shooting at. Bill noticed the kid crouched by the livery stable. He seemed to be holding off Stanton's men all on his lonesome. The kid waved when he saw Bill and then shot, taking one of the riders clean between the eyes. The man's head slung back, crimson spraying in the air while his horse bolted with the dead man hanging from the saddle.

Bill made for the kid, keeping low in the saddle while hot lead screamed all around him. As soon as he reached the livery stable he pulled on the reins and dived from the saddle, using his startled horse as cover while he slid across the ground, the dirt puffing up around him as slugs tore into it. As soon as it was able to, the horse galloped out of the main street, which had now become a war zone.

'Come on,' the kid shouted. 'I'll cover you.' The kid fired several times in quick succession and then ducked back down behind the livery stable, before immediately emerging and firing again.

Bill didn't need telling twice and, taking a deep breath and praying to some ancient Welsh deity, he made for the livery stable.

'We've got us a fight at last,' the kid said, seemingly delighted with the situation. 'Did you see that? I got Clemens.'

Bill stared at the kid, incredulously. Sam was dead, that much was certain, and Dutch's fate was still unknown, and yet the kid couldn't have been happier. The likelihood was that they could be killed at any moment and the kid was, for want of a better word, enjoying it.

'How many left out there?' Bill asked and filled the chambers of both of his Colts.

'Search me,' the kid said and peered around the corner of the building. He fired again. 'That's one less,' he said with a smile.

'Where's Dutch?'

'He's alive,' the kid said. 'But he sure ain't moving much.'

Bill lay down on his stomach and peered around the corner of the building. He could see Dutch lying on the boardwalk outside the hotel. There was a pool of blood around his head that was visible even to Bill and the man was almost perfectly still but for a twitching in one of his legs. He was still alive, but had lost a lot of blood and Bill knew that if he didn't get medical attention soon he would perish. Bill couldn't see any of Stanton's men but he knew they were out there somewhere. They had now all taken cover and their horses had scattered. There were maybe six men dead in the street.

'We've got to get to him,' Bill said, peering around the side of the stable. He had to quickly pull himself back behind the building when lead once again heated up the air.

'We're pinned down,' the kid said and once more peered around the side of the building. He spotted a man with a rifle in the top window and he took aim and fired. The shot was true and the man fell forward, out of the window and on to the ground below. A furious barrage answered the shot and the kid had to quickly duck back for cover.

Large chunks were torn out of the livery stable wall.

Bill took another look around the building. If he could make it across the street and get to Dutch he figured he could drag him into the hotel and make a stand from there. The trouble was he would present an easy target as he ran for the hotel.

There was no other way, though.

He couldn't just leave Dutch there.

He tried to place all of Stanton's men but it was impossible as they were keeping themselves out of sight. There were maybe six or seven men dead in the street and that included Sam, so by Bill's calculations that meant that there were at least fifteen men remaining out there, including Caleb Stanton.

'I'm going to have to try,' he said and pulled himself back under cover.

'That's crazy,'

'Aye,' Bill said. 'My *da* always said I was *twp*.'

The kid looked around them for a moment. 'If I break cover,' he said, 'Draw their fire — you may be able to pick a couple of them off. The more men we get the better the chance of getting to Dutch.'

It made sense but Bill thought it too much of a risk. 'What you got in mind?' he asked.

'See the well,' the kid pointed to the town well, which was situated some fifteen feet away. 'I reckon I can get to that if I move quick enough. There's cover there.'

Bill nodded.

'You need to be ready,' the kid said. 'They're gonna open fire immediately and you'll need to get as many as you can. I'll stay by the well a few minutes and then break cover again and run back here. They won't expect that.'

Again Bill nodded. He once again checked his Colts and got into a crouching position so he would be able to move as soon as the kid did.

'I'll go on three,' the kid said and filled the chamber of his own gun.

Again Bill nodded and mouthed a silent prayer.

'One,' the kid said.

Bill crossed himself.

'Two,' the kid said.

'Wait,' Bill grabbed the kid's arm.

The kid looked at him, puzzled.

'Before you go,' Bill said, 'I need to know.'

'Know what?'

'Just what did Caleb do to start all this? What did he do to your ma?'

The kid smiled. 'Sumbitch whistled at her,' he said.

'He whistled?'

The kid nodded. 'I'm gonna kill that bastard.'

'All this,' Bill was incredulous. He

couldn't believe what he was hearing. 'Everything we've been through. And all because some cowboy whistled at your mother?'

'It was the way he whistled at her,' the kid said and once again started his countdown. 'One.'

Bill shook his head, speechless.

'Two.'

Bill tensed and prepared himself to move.

'Three!' With that the kid made a break for it, leaping from the relative safety of the livery stable and making for the scant cover the well offered. Bullets spat up the ground at his feet as he ran.

Bill saw a man positioned in the jailhouse doorway and he shot, hitting the man in the gut and sending him sliding to the ground. Another fired at Bill and the Welshman dived back behind cover but not before noticing Caleb Stanton crouching down by the fence that ran alongside the newspaper office. Bill quickly broke cover and fired at Stanton before ducking back behind the livery stable.

He didn't think he had hit Stanton.

'You got one,' the kid shouted from his new position behind the well. 'That weren't too good, Welsh.'

Bill waved back to him.

'You count this time,' the kid yelled.

Bill nodded and refilled his guns.

'And try and get more of them.'

'I'll do my best to oblige,' Bill yelled back. The damn kid really did think this was all a game.

'Can you see Dutch?' Bill yelled.

The kid carefully lifted his head above the well and had to quickly duck back down when a bullet chipped the stone and whistled off somewhere.

'He's moving now,' the kid said. 'He's in shock. If he get's up he's dead.'

'One,' Bill yelled.

The kid nodded.

'Two.'

The kid holstered his weapon and pushed his hands into the dirt, bringing his legs up, crouching like an athlete.

'Three,' Bill yelled and broke cover, firing widely as the kid started back towards the livery stable.

The kid almost made it, too. He was no more than three or four steps from the livery stable when one of his legs seemed to betray him. The kid yelled and fell, reaching for the injured leg.

'I've been hit,' the kid yelled and said no more as he was hit again. This time the wound was fatal and entered the side of his head, throwing him sideways to where he came to rest, eyes open with what looked like a smile upon his face.

'No,' Bill yelled and foolishly stepped out of cover. He saw Bear taking aim from the hotel boardwalk and he fired, creating a grisly looking hole in the squat man's forehead. Next he shot towards Caleb but again missed when Stanton dived down behind the fence. There was another man on the hotel roof and Bill fired, taking him out.

Bill saw the hotel door open and noticed Martha come out. He looked at her for a moment, but a man taking aim from the jailhouse doorway took his attention. Bill aimed and fired in one fluid motion and the man was thrown back into the jailhouse. Bill watched as Martha bent to aid Dutch and started to drag him back towards the hotel door.

The sound of a bugle broke the air and Bill smiled. Thomson had finally returned and from the sound of it, he had brought the army with him.

There was no more gunfire; Stanton's men seemed to have decided on a cease-fire. Once again the bugle sounded and now the thunder of many galloping horses could be heard. Bill noticed Stanton's men coming out of hiding, their arms held above their heads. They had no appetite to continue the fight now that the army were coming.

Bill was just about to go to Martha and Dutch when he saw Caleb break cover and run towards the hotel.

'Watch out,' Bill shouted and started towards the hotel, but before the

Welshman could react Caleb had grabbed Martha and disappeared into the hotel with her.

Bill ran after them.

25

Bill went through the door quickly but immediately stopped dead. There before him stood Caleb and he held Martha tightly to him, the barrel of his Colt pressed beneath her chin.

'Take off your gun-belt,' Caleb ordered. 'Slowly or I'll blow this woman's head off.' Martha struggled in his arms but it was no good and Caleb merely held her tighter.

Bill unbuckled his gun-belt and allowed it to hang in one of his hands.

'Toss it away,' Caleb said. 'Over there.'

Bill threw it towards the door.

'Good,' Caleb said and pushed Martha away from him and then shot Bill.

The slug spun Bill around and threw him to the floor. A red-hot wave of agony sent shockwaves through his body and he gritted his teeth against the pain. He'd been hit in the side, the bullet passing straight through him, a flesh wound he guessed, but it hurt like hell.

Caleb smiled and took aim again, this time squaring the sights at Bill's head. Once again he pulled the trigger, but the pin came down on an empty chamber.

'No matter,' Caleb said and tossed the Schofield aside. He pulled a vicious looking hunting knife from the scabbard on the back of his belt. 'I'm gonna slit your throat,' he said and advanced on Bill.

Bill tried to get up but he couldn't. His shirt was now saturated with blood and he started to feel light headed. He felt dizzy but fought the feeling, willing himself not to lose consciousness as Caleb came and stood over him.

Caleb smiled evilly and then knelt down and grabbed Bill's head with one hand while the other brought the vicious looking knife into play.

Bill's hand reached inside his shirt and he pulled out one of his knitting needles. He rammed it upwards with all his strength and it entered Caleb's left eye, bursting the eyeball, which spurted out optical fluid and blood. With that, Caleb dropped the knife and the weight of his own body drove the needle into his brain.

Unconsciousness finally overtook Bill and he slipped away, Caleb's lifeless body atop him.

26

Time sure did fly, Bill thought as he realized it had been almost a year since the shoot-out with Caleb Stanton. A full twelve months had gone past, and he was still here and guessed he would remain so for some time to come. He had nowhere else to go and besides, these days he had ties to the town. For one thing he wore the tin star himself and took pride in his role as town sheriff. And for another he had a wife, a good woman, and he had not looked back since marrying Martha almost ten months ago. From time to time he would think of his beloved Blodwen back in the home country but he kept these thoughts to himself. That had been another life.

Bill patted the side of his horse's head gently as they approached the town boundaries. He took this ride every afternoon, called it his patrol. He would circle the town and then ride out to the old Stanton place before doing the whole thing in reverse. He smiled as he reached the outskirts of the town and saw the welcome sign.

It always tickled him.

WELCOME TO WILLIAMSTOWN.

We do hope that you have enjoyed reading this large print book.

Did you know that all of our titles are available for purchase?

We publish a wide range of high quality large print books including:
Romances, Mysteries, Classics
General Fiction
Non Fiction and Westerns

Special interest titles available in large print are:
The Little Oxford Dictionary
Music Book, Song Book
Hymn Book, Service Book

Also available from us courtesy of Oxford University Press:
Young Readers' Dictionary
(large print edition)
Young Readers' Thesaurus
(large print edition)

For further information or a free brochure, please contact us at:
Ulverscroft Large Print Books Ltd.,
The Green, Bradgate Road, Anstey,
Leicester, LE7 7FU, England.
Tel: (00 44) 0116 236 4325
Fax: (00 44) 0116 234 0205

Other titles in the
Linford Western Library:

KILL SLAUGHTER

Henry Remington

When a California train is robbed of
$30,000, and two Pinkerton detec-
tives are killed, bounty hunter James
Slaughter rides to investigate. But a
cloud of fear hangs over the railroad
town of Visalia, and even the judge
is running scared. Beaten up, jailed
and framed by the sheriff's deputies,
Slaughter survives assassination at-
tempts — but is hit by still more
trouble as a vicious range war erupts
on the prairie . . .